"I wouldn't be █████ ███ option."

Eric lifted his gaze █████ ██████ ████ briefly.

"I know." She puffed out the breath she didn't realize she'd been holding. Rounding the desk, she laid a hand on his shoulder. "Come on. I'll walk you to your car. Rest today and get geared up. You're no good to your sister if you land yourself in the hospital."

Without a word, he stood and let her usher him out the door and into the lobby. At the exterior door, Morgan called over her shoulder to another ranger, "Be back in a minute."

He waved her away with a quick glance. Yeah, nobody knew that, to her, Eric was so much more than a grieving family member.

They stepped into the warmth of a May morning, and Morgan ushered him to the end of the sidewalk near the parking lot. "Where's your car?"

Eric aimed the key fob at a gunmetal-gray Jeep Wrangler near the end of the first row, pressing the key fob.

And the world exploded.

Valerie Hansen was thirty when she awoke to the presence of the Lord in her life and turned to Jesus. She now lives in a renovated farmhouse on the breathtakingly beautiful Ozark Plateau of Arkansas and is privileged to share her personal faith by telling the stories of her heart for Love Inspired. Life doesn't get much better than that!

Jodie Bailey writes novels about freedom and the heroes who fight for it. Her novel *Crossfire* won a 2015 RT Reviewers' Choice Best Book Award. She is convinced a camping trip to the beach with her family, a good cup of coffee and a great book can cure all ills. Jodie lives in North Carolina with her husband, her daughter and two dogs.

CANYON
STANDOFF

VALERIE HANSEN
AND
JODIE BAILEY

LOVE INSPIRED SUSPENSE
INSPIRATIONAL ROMANCE

LOVE INSPIRED® SUSPENSE
INSPIRATIONAL ROMANCE

Recycling programs
for this product may
not exist in your area.

ISBN-13: 978-1-335-40274-5

Canyon Standoff

Copyright © 2020 by Harlequin Books S.A.

Canyon Under Siege
Copyright © 2020 by Valerie Whisenand

Missing in the Wilderness
Copyright © 2020 by Jodie Bailey

This edition published by arrangement with Harlequin Books S.A.

For questions and comments about the quality of this book,
please contact us at CustomerService@Harlequin.com.

Love Inspired
22 Adelaide St. West, 40th Floor
Toronto, Ontario M5H 4E3, Canada
www.Harlequin.com

Printed in U.S.A.

CONTENTS

CANYON UNDER SIEGE

Valerie Hansen

To national park rangers, the brave men and women who stand ready to pull the rest of us back from the brink when we get into trouble after ignoring their sensible advice. God bless 'em all.

From the end of the earth I will cry unto thee,
when my heart is overwhelmed: lead me to the rock
that is higher than I. For thou hast been a shelter for me,
and a strong tower from the enemy.
—*Psalm* 61:2-3

ONE

Storm clouds darkened the north rim of the Grand Canyon, casting ominous shadows into the abyss. Pounding desert rain was threatening to sweep across the miles of open canyon and deluge the south rim helipad before rangers of the Search and Rescue team could fully mobilize.

Holly trembled with trepidation. She knew what was going to happen when Gabe realized who she was. And then there he was, jogging toward her. The one person who set her nerves on edge while also bringing assurance of safety, even while dangling from a rope suspended below a helicopter or rappelling down a cliff. Except she was no teenage novice seasonal volunteer anymore, she was Agent Holly Forbes of the FBI. And she was there for one purpose: to do her job, not because she'd once had a foolish crush on National Park Ranger Gabe McClellan.

Wind was picking up, whipping strands of her long, dark hair across her face and stinging her cheeks, but that was the least of her worries. She stood tall and still, expecting some kind of reaction when Gabe recognized her. Instead, he passed by as if she were simply in his way and began shouting orders to his men—and one woman—as they stowed their gear aboard the chopper.

The vibration of her cell phone startled her. Pressing it to her ear, she tried to shelter it from the wind with her body. "What? I can't hear you!"

A firm hand grasped her elbow. Her eyes locked with Gabe's for an instant before he tapped the side of his flight helmet and shouted, "I just got the full report by radio, Agent Forbes. Let's go."

"Are you sure?"

His dark eyes narrowed slightly as he nodded but that was the only sign he was perturbed. If she hadn't known him so well in the past she'd have missed the reaction.

"Yes." Keeping temporary hold, he urged her toward the chopper. "I'll give you a headset and brief everybody once we're in the air. In case you haven't noticed, there's a storm brewing."

"Well, *yeah*." Holly had to hustle to keep pace with him. "It'll be safer below the rim."

"Usually is." Gabe handed her up to two other rangers, who hoisted her aboard and made room for her. "Belt in."

Still, he'd given no indication that he remembered her, whereas she would have been able to pick him out of a crowd of thousands. So much for the way he'd made her feel so special when she'd worked in the park. Their brief summer acquaintance had obviously meant a lot more to her than it had to him.

The whomp of the blades sped up until the sound was a deafening roar. They were airborne. Holly felt an imaginary hole in the pit of her stomach and grabbed the edge of the seat as the pilot banked to the left before straightening out. Then the loaded chopper passed over the edge and dropped into the magnificent canyon.

She'd often wondered how something so beautiful could claim so many lives, and she'd come to the conclusion survival depended on respect. If hikers or other visitors to Grand Canyon National Park paid attention to the rangers, stayed on the trails and were properly equipped and hydrated during the blazing summers, they lived.

She shivered. Disregard the warnings or wander from safe trails and the canyon was apt to swallow you up. She'd seen it happen. And she never wanted to witness that kind of pointless death again.

Her gaze darted from the scenery outside to Gabe's face. Stoic and fully in control, he epitomized the perfect park ranger. How he could work Search and Rescue and keep his cool despite the fact they couldn't hope to save everyone was more than amazing to Holly—it was terribly, terribly sad.

Gabe tried to stay focused on the task at hand, yet something about the serious FBI agent kept niggling at his subconscious. The park was very attractive to athletic young people looking for a challenge or just unwinding after rough college finals, so there was a chance this agent reminded him of one of those green kids. It had surprised him when she hadn't balked at climbing aboard the chopper with his team. It would have pleased him more to have made this rescue without extra baggage but that couldn't be helped this time. Orders to include her had come from above.

Gabe tapped the side of his helmet again and began talking to his SAR team. "The latest news from Spirit Ranch Station is bad. We have one ranger down and two missing." He had to hold up his hand to stop questions. "I haven't been given particulars that make a lot of sense. We have conflicting reports, at best."

"What are our plans?" someone asked.

"Rescue, above all." He eyed the FBI agent. "After that, maybe our ride-along FBI agent can fill us in."

"Armed and dangerous to begin with," Holly reported. "At least three men plus their driver fled Las Vegas after a drug cartel meeting went bad." She paused and sobered even more. "They took out two of my fellow agents. One of them is clinging to life in a hospital right now."

"How did they end up here?"

"That's unknown. It's believed they commandeered a boat and were into the canyon before they realized their mistake. We were setting up to capture them, as you probably heard, when they went ashore at Spirit Ranch Station and took hostages."

"I'm glad your bosses were smart enough to pull the FBI and sheriff's helicopters out when they did," Gabe said sagely. "A pilot who isn't familiar with air currents and the heat index inside the canyon is a real risk."

"I know." A slight smile lifted the corners of her mouth. Recognition dawned on Gabe as she said, "You can thank *me* for that one."

"That *is* where I know you from!" Gabe grinned over at her. "People, Agent Forbes was one of our summer interns." Her first name remained elusive, so he paused in the hope she'd provide it.

"My nickname was Christmas when I worked here. You can all call me Holly if you want."

"That's right. Holly Forbes, aka Christmas." How could he have forgotten? Perhaps it was less a matter of forgetting than of not recognizing the woman she had become. The laughing, lighthearted temp he'd met nine, maybe ten years ago bore only a faint resemblance to the somber person she was now. Had life hardened her that much? he wondered. It was possible. It was also possible she was the kind of agent who could focus so well on the job at hand she was able to set aside personal feelings. That could be a valuable asset.

Gabe was jarred from his thoughts by a sudden banking of the chopper. The pilot yelled, "Taking fire!"

Holly instinctively ducked while the armed rangers went into action. Rifles appeared. Men took up positions at the open side door, waiting for their pilot to give them a target. She, too, was armed but not with anything that would reach the ground accurately. Considering the evasive action the helo was taking, she doubted anybody was going to be able to successfully return fire.

Gabe shouldered her away from the door. "Stay back."

"I am." She eyed him critically. "Anybody who takes his safety harness off at a time like this is a fool."

Scowling, he broadcast, "Anybody hit?"

A garbled chorus of assurance was a relief. Holly took a second to assess herself. She'd been slightly wounded several times in the line of duty and knew the shock of a bullet could dull the pain enough that an injured person might not realize damage had been done right away.

"How about you, FBI?" Gabe asked.

"I'm in one piece as far as I know."

There was no need to tell the veteran chopper jockey what to do. He was already taking his passengers higher and wider to get out of range. Bright sun from directly overhead glinted off something below. A rifle barrel? She grabbed at Gabe and pointed. "Look!"

"Where?"

"Down there. I know I saw a flash of light, like a reflection." Holly made a face of disgust and then sighed. "It's gone. Sorry."

"All right," Gabe shouted into his mic. "Plan B. We put down a few men in the canyon as close as we can without getting shot."

"Brilliant. Now we know how you got to be senior ranger," someone quipped.

Gabe huffed. "Right. Law enforcement only." He pointed. "Hough and Broadstreet are trained medics, too. What about you, FBI?"

"Fully trained," Holly assured him. "I know how to rappel, too."

"Good, because I'd hate to have you hanging on the end of a rope like a panicked kid afraid to drop into a swimming hole."

"If you really remembered me, you'd know I don't panic," she countered.

"I hope you're better at taking orders than you used to be," he said. "If memory serves, you almost drowned trying to rescue a kid from some rapids because you failed to secure yourself before diving in."

"Yes, and I learned my lesson," Holly said, hoping her face wasn't as red as it felt. "You gave me the lecture of my life in front of all my peers."

"Let's hope it took," Gabe said. "Challenging nature can get you killed."

Holly quirked a smile and glanced out as they rose above reddish rock cliffs and deep crevasses. "The only nature that scares me is human nature."

Another bright flash in the canyon below was followed by the sound of another rifle shot.

Pressing her back tight to her seat Holly added, "Especially when somebody is shooting at me!"

TWO

Rain fell in sheets as Holly, Gabe, the medics and several others shouldered their packs and started to hike downriver toward the besieged ranger station. Gabe had sent their chopper back to the south rim to wait. Hovering over the unforgiving canyon wasn't wise, particularly during a storm, and by the time he needed an airlift the worst of the weather should be over.

As the thump of the rotors faded, Holly spoke to the group. "One advantage we have is that these men we're after aren't outdoorsmen. They're the business-suit type. Totally out of their element here. As soon as we get under cover, I'll show you the enhanced photos from the casino security cams."

"You're sure of who they are?"

"Reasonably sure, although we're still working on positive IDs. How far are we from Spirit? I wouldn't want them to slip in among regular tourists and get away."

"In this weather?" Gabe wiped his wet face with one hand. "Even the mules are smart enough to refuse to go outside."

She laughed softly. "What does that say about us?"

"That we picked challenging jobs."

"Understatement."

"I hope that jacket is waterproof," he commented, eyeing her.

"I doubt anything would keep me dry in this monsoon. At least it's a lot warmer down here than it was up on the rim."

"We'll all be sorry about that soon enough unless we get the job done and evacuate."

"Yeah."

Gabe trekked for another fifteen minutes before he halted and drew his group into a huddle. "The valley's widening out. We'll be able to see Spirit Station soon. That means they'll also be able to see us, particularly now that the rain has stopped. We need to split up, make separate targets." Pausing, he looked deliberately at Holly. "Except for you, FBI. You'll stay with me."

When she rolled her eyes, he knew he was in for trouble. Hoping she'd follow orders if he ignored her reaction, he signaled to the medics to go right while he and Holly tended left and a small group headed straight in. His satisfaction with her compliance was short-lived. Although she did start out with him, her path kept drifting further and further afield.

Considering the likelihood that a shout would echo and might be overheard, Gabe carried on instead. His main concern had to be his injured colleagues and any innocent bystanders who had been harmed or were otherwise in jeopardy. What he had to remember, if he expected to stay focused, was that Holly Forbes was no novice. She'd arrived properly outfitted and had hiked these trails before. Diverting his attention could cost him dearly.

"Which is exactly what I'm going to tell her, first chance I get," Gabe muttered. Thoughts of her caused him to glance to the side. His jaw dropped open. Not only was the agent in full view, she was waving her arms overhead and jumping up and down. She might as well announce their presence with a loudspeaker!

Red mud splashed as Gabe jogged toward her, furious. At least she wasn't screaming. That was something.

Gruff and angry, he grabbed her shoulders to still her. "What do you think you're doing?"

"Getting your attention," she said, breathless.

"If you'd stayed with me the way I told you to, you wouldn't have to jump around like you had scorpions in your boots."

"Hush! Listen. Somebody's calling for help."

"I don't hear a thing."

"Well, I do. I did. It came from over that way. Maybe on the Kaibab Trail."

Gabe released her. "Not from the direction of the station? Okay. I'll radio the rim and have a second search team stand by to respond when we give the all clear."

"That'll take too long. The voice sounded like a woman or a child. If they really need help, somebody should go to them immediately."

"Nobody else is coming down here until we're sure the area is secure. Period. It would be crazy to add any more people to the bunch we already have to worry about."

"Fine. I get it. I do. But…"

"Tell you what," Gabe said. "Suppose you check out the noise you heard and I'll keep my team with me. You can radio us if you locate a victim, and we'll calculate their position based on yours. If I can send help at that time, I will."

He understood how torn she was. Not only did it show in her face, he wasn't feeling good about splitting forces. If he'd trained with Holly recently, he might be making a different decision, but the way he saw it, sending her off on her own might be for the best. She'd perform a necessary service and not be underfoot while he and his rangers tried to liberate Spirit Station. Plus, she had enough experience at the Grand Canyon to stay out of trouble as long as she thought with her brain and not her heart.

As she turned away he said, "Holly, wait." The words were out of his mouth before he'd taken time to think through what he wanted to tell her.

"Yes?"

"I don't have time to go over all the safety rules so I hope you remember them."

"You mean like 'don't dive into any raging rivers without a rope anchoring me to shore'?"

"Yeah. Like that." His radio crackled. The others were almost in position and not seeing any activity in or around the station. "Look, I've gotta go. If you hear the code word, *vacation*, that means change radio frequencies to confuse the crooks. I don't have the list with me but you can find us if you scan." Concern welled within him. He started to pat her shoulder, then thought better of it.

"One promise?" she asked.

"What?"

"Let's keep this little side trip to ourselves. I wasn't sent here to rescue lost hikers. I was sent to capture fugitives. The only reason I'm not going with you right now is because you have them cornered and I'm really not necessary. Yet."

"Agreed. If I get the drop on them before you get back, I'll hold them for you so you get all the credit. No extra charge."

Smiling, she offered her right hand. Gabe took it, meaning only to shake the way he would to seal any bargain.

A tingle raced up his arm the moment their hands joined, leaving a wake of surprising warmth and awareness. He didn't have to ask if she felt it, too. Her dark eyes were wide, lashes damp with rain, and she seemed as startled as he was.

A tug freed his hold and she took off, breaking into an easy lope along the more even ground of the canyon bottom. Gabe turned to face the besieged ranger station. He could see knots of tourists in the distance. Some summer volunteers and river concessionaires were holding back crowds as best they could and a couple of leathery-faced mule skinners had mounted up and positioned themselves along the broader approaches and the footbridge entrance in order to limit public access.

"This is going to work," Gabe told himself, adding "Thank You, God" to his earlier prayers.

He was reaching for his radio to coordinate with his team when there was a loud bang followed by the characteristic whine of a bullet. His head whipped around. He scanned for the shooter, saw no one, then turned toward the place he'd last seen Holly.

She'd disappeared!

THREE

Holly had hit the dirt on her stomach the instant she'd realized shots were being fired. Heart racing, pulse pounding in her ears, she waited for the next bullet. It didn't come.

Slowly, cautiously, she rose, keeping her loaded backpack between her and the general direction of the ranger station, where she thought the noise had originated. With the echoes up and down the canyon, it was hard to be certain, but given the drama currently unfolding at Spirit Ranch and the station nearby, it made sense.

She wiped muddy, sandy hands on her jeans and held her breath to listen, wondering if her wisest move would be to try to return to Gabe. The rain was moving on and the air was clear. Clean. Except for her continued hammering heartbeats, the canyon was silent.

And then she heard it. A call for help. And another. The voice was high and reedy. She'd been right! This victim was a woman or a child. Or one of each. Were they lost? Injured? Only a personal investigation would tell.

Her radio crackled. She grabbed it, noticing that her hand was shaking slightly. "Forbes."

"You okay, FBI?"

"Yeah. Muddy but fine. I ducked, just in case. You?"

"Same. I'm going to need a *vacation* when this is over."

"Me, too. I can still hear the lost hiker calling for help. I'm headed that way."

"Copy. Take care."

"Always," Holly replied.

Gabe had given the code word. There was no telling how often the rangers were going to change their radio signals so she'd wait until she needed to talk to them before fiddling with the settings on her radio. She knew from experience that even the strongest satellite signals could be unreliable inside the canyon and using cell phones was impossible. When park visitors meant to get back to nature, they had no trouble doing it in the bottom of the 277-mile-long Grand Canyon.

If they had been John Muir or John Wesley Powell, they'd have come prepared the way she and the rangers had. The problem was, many vacationers disregarded sensible warnings because they thought they were smarter or more physically fit than average. That was when the canyon took its toll, sometimes fatally.

Fan-shaped soil and rock deposited by erosion at the base of a narrow slot canyon slowed Holly's progress while rock formations channeled the calls for help like a stone megaphone. Leaning into the climb, she pressed on, slipping on wet rocks, which caused her to slide here and there. No other footprints showed, but they wouldn't after the hard rain.

Holly scanned overhead, checking for storm clouds. None were visible. That was a good sign, although the steep rise of the canyon side did block a lot of her view. She cupped her hands around her mouth and shouted up the steep-sided rift. "Hello? Anybody there?"

To her relief and delight, a woman called, "Yes! Up here. Help!"

"Hang on. I'm on my way. Can you come down to me?"

"No. I think my son has a broken leg."

There was no point asking why the mother and child had left known trails and ventured off on their own. It happened all the time. It was as if the serpentine slits leading off the main canyon summoned hikers, promising to reveal marvelous secrets that obedient visitors might miss. Holly understood the appeal. She'd had her share of adventures as a teen, although she'd never needed to be helped to find her way back.

Sometimes she'd discovered hidden pools of rainwater that were a lot warmer for swimming than the icy river. Sometimes there were ancient rock markings made by Native Americans who had revered the canyon and treated it with utmost respect.

Holly continued to pull herself up, climbing water-smoothed, rippling rocks that were layered like the stacks of pancakes served in the Spirit Ranch lodge. Her stomach growled at the thought. She ignored it. Each corner she turned was one closer to the injured little boy. If he wasn't too big, maybe she and his mother could carry him out once she'd splinted his leg, assuming it was actually broken. As soon as she had assessed the situation she'd radio Gabe and fill him in.

Grunting with the effort, she hoisted herself over a wide outcropping and finally saw them. The woman began to weep loudly. "Oh, thank you, Ranger."

"I'm not a ranger," Holly said, "but I used to work here as a volunteer." She sidled past the mother to get to the child. His face was beet red, his breathing shallow.

"When was the last time you gave him water?" Holly asked, checking him over quickly.

"We ran out. I was sure I had enough but after he got hurt, we used it all up. I've been calling and calling. Where are all the day trippers?"

"It's a long story." Holly lowered her pack and got out one of her bottles of water, offering some to the child. "Here. Don't drink it too fast or it might make you sick."

She turned the job of dispensing sips of water over to the mother. "We need to get you and…"

The mother supplied names. "He's Robert and I'm Renee."

"I'm Holly. We need to get Robert and you out of here and back to the first aid station on the rim."

"What about Robbie's leg?"

"I don't think it's broken. But I'll stabilize it just in case. Then you and I will pack him out."

"I can't carry him and climb. I tried. The rocks are too loose. I kept slipping."

As frustrated as she was, Holly knew better than to argue with a frantic parent. What she needed was backup. What she wanted was Gabe McClellan. However, any muscle would do in a pinch. Too bad other park rangers had managed to stop most tourists from descending. The only visitors left were those who had begun their journey before the trail was blocked or inveterate hikers who had managed to sneak past the barricades.

Pebbles rained down on them from an upper trail, catching Holly by surprise. "Hey! Anybody up there? We need some help here," she shouted.

Too close to the canyon walls to see very far above, she was happy to draw one man's attention. He peered over the edge of the loop of trail directly above them.

"Can you join us and help? I need to rig a way for this child and his mother to be rescued."

"Why me?"

She merely smiled and shrugged. "You're handy. I really need some muscle and the rangers are busy."

"They are, huh?"

"Yes, they are. Can we count on you?"

"How do I know you didn't hurt the kid yourself? Maybe push him or something?"

"Because I'm an officer of the law," Holly said, so fed up with this hiker she could scream.

"I suppose you can prove that?"

"Yes." She pulled out her FBI identification. "Can you see this from up there?"

"Good enough. Why didn't you call the rangers to rescue him? They do this kind of stuff all the time, right?"

"Because they're dealing with a crisis of their own."

"Okay, okay. How do I get there without falling off this cliff?"

"You should be able to sit down and slide to us. Just use your feet and hands as brakes so you don't overshoot. Once you're here, we can carry the boy out at the bottom and make an evacuation plan."

His "Okay" sounded reluctant. "Step back so you're not in my way in case I can't stop."

Holly was so relieved, she had little else on her mind. Moving the mother and child aside, she supported Robbie's injured side and used her own back to shield him from pebbles that might be dislodged.

The stranger's descent was noisy and would have been dusty, too, if the rain had not recently dampened the loose rock and sand.

He landed with a thud just behind her. She straightened, preparing to offer to shake his hand, then froze. Her supposed hiker was wearing dress shoes and slacks. There was no suit jacket over his soggy, dirty, long-sleeved shirt, but that hardly mattered. The instant she looked into his squinting eyes, she knew.

She'd seen his face in the grainy security footage.

She was in deep trouble.

FOUR

Gabe devoted his full attention to the planned siege until receiving orders from National Park Service headquarters to hold his position. A trained FBI negotiator was on the way and the powers that be wanted the rangers on scene to defer to him or her.

That suited Gabe just fine as long as the FBI hurried. He'd watched storm clouds pass his location and begin to shadow the craggy, mile-high walls, showing that it was still too soon to chance another flight. Until someone had actually stood in the bottom of the gorge the way he was now, it was impossible to fully appreciate the ruggedness and distance involved. Same went for the clouds swiftly crossing the rim and disappearing out of sight. Their actual positions over land could be very deceptive.

A niggling sense of impending disaster kept him on edge. Where was Holly? He switched his radio back to the original setting and called her. "Status report, Forbes."

Nothing. The airwaves were silent. He tried again. "McClellan to Forbes. Report."

Sounding breathless, she finally said, "I'm in a really cramped canyon offshoot of Kaibab Trail with a mother and child."

"Narrow? How far up does it go?"

"That's unknown."

"Be advised. The storm is still over the south rim. I can see heavy rain falling. Watch for runoff."

"Copy."

Someone else broke in. "Flash flooding reported all along the rim, north and south. Evacuation recommended."

That was enough for Gabe. He ran up to one of the familiar mule skinners and quickly explained his need for the animal.

No questions were asked. None were needed. The other man dismounted and passed him the reins. Gabe took control. He'd spent plenty of leisure hours with the mules, partly because he missed ranch life in Texas. Chosen for strong constitutions and docile temperaments, the mules were a lot more intelligent and athletic than they usually appeared. With the right rider aboard, a Grand Canyon National Park mule could be almost as fast as a good horse and a lot more sensible.

He tightened his knees and gave his mount an easy kick. Ears laid back, it bunched under him and sprang forward as if starting a race. Its running gait was a little choppier than that of most horses but Gabe needed its superior stamina.

He leaned into the wind, guiding the mule to retrace his own path to the place where he'd last seen Holly. As he had feared, there was no sign of her.

"Forbes!" he broadcast. "Did you hear the warning? Climb."

Radio static set every nerve in his body tingling with apprehension. She must have heard. She had to have. Any other scenario was unacceptable.

Mule and rider took off through the rocks and brush. Gabe knew roughly where Holly was. That would have to do. The danger to her and the tourists would be brief, yet there was no escape from the rushing waters other than taking to higher ground. Outrunning the deluge was as impossible as trying to pace the special tourist train that came out of Williams. Once a flood started, it was unstoppable, gaining strength and gathering debris every second.

Gabe nudged the mule for more speed and shouted into the radio, "Holly! Climb!"

Part of Holly felt in charge of the situation despite the fact that the well-dressed thug had gotten the drop on her, now had possession of her sidearm and was waving his own gun around like a toy.

"Are you listening? Did you hear that?" she asked, surprised to hear so much command in her voice. "We can't stand around down here until you decide what you're going to do. We need to escape."

"So you say. How do I know this isn't a trick? You're the expert, not me." He gestured at the handheld radio. "Maybe you and your boyfriend worked this out just to nab me."

"And planted an injured little boy in your path?" She rolled her eyes. "Oh, sure. Like I knew you were going to be on that exact branch of the trail." Frowning, she paused. "How did you get up there anyway? I thought you and your buddies were holed up at the ranger station." The minute those words were out of her mouth, she realized her error.

"You know who I am."

"Everybody does."

"I don't think so, lady. I thought you were kidding when you said you were a cop. Give me that radio. And let me see your ID again."

As she held out the radio and slowly reached for her badge wallet, she began issuing orders. "Okay. Here's what's going to happen—unless you want to bring the whole federal government down on your head. I'm going to pick up Robbie, and Renee and I are going to scale that wall. You're going to let us, and if I were you, I'd come along."

The thug was squinting at her FBI credentials and muttering to himself as if he wasn't hearing anything she said.

Holly handed her backpack to the weeping woman, helped the child to his feet, bent low in front of him and said, "Put your arms around my neck and your legs around my waist, like you're my pack. Understand?"

"Uh-huh," he whimpered. "My leg hurts."

"We have to climb to higher ground. Like superheroes. Can you be really brave for me?"

She felt him nod. His grip tightened. Placing her boots carefully, she started up the slippery sides of the canyon, still urging everyone to follow. "Step where I do and look for handholds as you go, Renee. Don't be too picky, just hurry."

In the background she heard a hum becoming a roar. The acoustics of the narrow fissure where they were trapped amplified the sound, making it all the more terrifying.

"Climb! Faster!" Holly shouted. "It's coming."

A quick glance behind told her that Renee had found the courage to follow. Standing in the bottom of the rocky draw, the thug had her gun in one hand, her radio in his other, and was staring at the roiling flash flood waters as they tumbled toward him, a wall of red mud, rock and death.

Holly kept scrambling, praying all the way that they were high enough to escape being swept away by the torrent. Every step was punctuated by a fresh "Please, Jesus. Please…"

Gabe heard static on his radio, then a background roar, then a strangled scream. Every nerve in his body fired in response.

"Holly!"

Reacting to his rider's panic, the mule kicked, nearly unseating Gabe. "Easy, boy. Easy."

He regained control of both his emotions and his mount. They were almost there. A trickle of dirty, reddish-brown water marked the path. The mule tossed his head, took the bit in his teeth and literally leaped to the side.

Gabe hung on, knowing what was happening. Self-preservation had gripped the intelligent animal and it was fleeing impending death at breakneck speed, carrying him to higher ground whether he wanted to go or not.

His heart plummeted. "Oh, Holly, what have you done?"

As the mule reached a small plateau, it slowed. Its sides were heaving, its nostrils flared. Gabe trusted the wise equine. They were out of danger.

Below, where they had stood only moments before, the ground was alive with roiling, cascading mud. If Holly and the family she'd been trying to help hadn't reached high ground in time, they'd surely have been swallowed by the flash flood waters.

It was over in mere minutes. Debris remained, as did knee-deep, slippery mud, but the terrifying movement had nearly ceased. He leaned down and patted the breathless mule's neck. "Extra rations for you when we get back," he said tenderly. "I just wish you'd been a few minutes faster."

Heavyhearted, Gabe scanned the high, layered rocks around him, looking for people he didn't expect to see. He knew Holly. If she couldn't successfully rescue the hikers, she was likely to have remained with them, struggling until the last moment. That was just the kind of person she was.

His gaze misted so badly he had trouble focusing. Not only had he failed her, she maight have given her life on his watch. Yet how could he, in good conscience, have stopped her from going? She had the skills to help. The knowledge to lead everyone to safety. So had she succeeded? If only she'd answer his radio calls he'd know.

Perched on the side of a steep grade several hundred yards away, he spotted a blob of bright-colored clothing. Holly had been wearing green and gray, like the rest of his team, but perhaps these were the hikers she'd heard calling for aid.

Gabe straightened in the saddle, reins tightening, and began waving one arm.

An answering wave encouraged him.

He raised the radio so whoever was over there could see it. A second figure, this time in green, stepped up on a higher rock and waved with both arms. The signal was so familiar it nearly brought a sob of relief.

Praise God! Holly was alive!

FIVE

Breathless yet elated, Holly took off her damp jacket and used it to continue a broad wave at the man on the mule. It couldn't be Gabe. He was up to his eyeballs in a siege at the ranger station. But that rider definitely reminded her of him.

She smiled to herself. Joy at having saved the lives of the boy and his mother was tempered by the loss of the foolish criminal. If only he had listened.

The man on the higher ground was waving something. It took her a few seconds to guess it might be a hand-held radio. She spread both arms wide, palms up, hands empty, and shouted, "No radio!"

Had he heard her? Chances weren't good. She cupped her hands around her mouth, filled her lungs and gave it all the power she had. "No! Radio!"

An echoing answer followed. "All okay?"

"Yes!"

That seemed to suffice. The rider turned the mule and began urging it down the hill into the gorge. Holly didn't like him doing that but she also knew it was going to be hours before she and her companions would be safe trying to walk out. In her opinion, having help arrive on a sure-footed mule was a lot better than any knight in shining armor on a white horse would have been.

That silly image made her smile. So did the prospect of rescue. Later, a recovery team would have to start searching for the crook who had been buried beneath thousands of gallons of water and sediment. Most such victims were eventually located, particularly if there had been witnesses to the tragedy. In the case of this man, the authorities would definitely want to positively identify him, especially if he was associated with the criminals now holding rangers hostage, as she'd assumed.

The rider passed out of her sight below so she rejoined Renee and Robbie. "Somebody on a mule is coming for us."

The woman acted as if she was in shock but the child brightened. "I get to ride? Mama wouldn't let me before."

"Yes, you get to ride," Holly told him. "I don't think we all will fit in the saddle but you definitely will."

"Hooray!"

The innocence of youth made Holly smile again. This child lived in the present, eager for new challenges and open to the world, a lot like her poor sister had been. Thoughts of Ivy sobered her. Losing her only sibling at the hands of a killer had shaped the lives of their whole family from that day forward. Only she, Holly Forbes, had turned her grief into something positive. Other mourners close to Ivy, for instance their parents, had given up on life, divorced and gone their separate ways.

Pensive, she sighed. Hunting down criminals and making them pay was her reason for living. It was who she had become—the person she had created out of the ashes of loss—and that image was what kept her going. What made her so good at her job. It was also what had led her to break away from Gabe and the rangers to rescue these helpless folks. Her goal was to save as many lives as possible, even at the risk of her own. It didn't matter that she had been told she was trying in vain to atone for not saving her sister. What if she was? The important fact was that she had already preserved many lives and had vowed to continue for as long as she was able. Period. Nothing else took precedence. Not even her own safety.

As Gabe urged the mule up the canyon, he allowed it to pick its own trail. Very seldom did it falter and it never went all the way down despite hidden hazards. If he'd been on foot, or even on horseback, he wouldn't have attempted this climb.

He patted the mule's lathered neck again. "Good boy. That's it. Keep going. We're almost there."

The long grayish-brown ears were held forward, rotating like antennae in search of a stronger signal. They perked up even more when Gabe heard someone call, "Over here!"

He rounded a corner and looked up. Grinned. So happy he could hardly contain himself, he shouted, "Hello. Need a ride?"

"Gabe?" Holly's jaw dropped, then snapped closed. "What are you...? What about the...?" She laughed. "Never mind. Just get us out of here."

"Gladly."

Maneuvering the stalwart mule into position, he waited while the others climbed down to him. "Where's your radio?"

"It's a long story," Holly said. She lifted the child by his waist and handed him over. "He needs to ride with you."

"You women can ride, too. I'll walk."

"Not if we ever expect to get back to Spirit Station. I've never driven a mule and neither have my new friends. I asked them. Looks like you're in charge of transportation."

"I can walk and lead him," Gabe offered, settling the boy in front of him so he could more easily dismount.

"What about the problem in Spirit? Is it resolved already?"

He shook his head, assessing the civilians and wondering how much they knew. When his gaze met Holly's and she nodded, he assumed she'd explained. "We're still waiting for negotiators from Las Vegas. They were delayed by the storm but they should be on scene very soon."

"Then you need to be there," Holly said flatly. "I'll hold on to the pack straps on the saddle and pull myself along behind. I'm already so muddy it won't make any difference and we'll make better time that way."

Gabe eyed both women. "That might not be necessary. We just don't want to overload the mule." He bent over the boy. "What's your name, little buddy?"

"Robbie."

"Okay, Ranger Robbie. You sit really still while I help your mama and my friend Holly. Okay?"

"Okay!"

He reached down. "Give me your hand, ma'am."

Renee didn't look eager to board the mule. "I'm all dirty. I'll get everything muddy."

"Won't be the first time." His hand remained outstretched. "I need to get back to Spirit ASAP. Please?"

Lifting her and swinging her up behind him, Gabe frowned and studied Holly. "How much do you weigh?"

"I beg your pardon?"

He chuckled. "It's not a personal question, Christmas. I was adding up the pounds to decide if you could ride, too. These guys carry heavy packs as well as people and they do it on narrow trails. If I don't push him too hard, I think my big-eared friend can carry us all without hurting himself."

She muttered a number. Gabe couldn't resist commenting, "That much? Wow!"

She took a playful whack at his leg and spooked the mule enough that Gabe had to settle it again before she could mount.

"If you're done scaring the livestock, Agent Forbes, I suggest we get a move on. I really do belong with my team."

"Yes, sir, Mr. Ranger. Sorry, Mr. Ranger. It won't happen again."

Laughing softly, he gave her a hand up behind him and Renee. "Okay, Robbie. You can help me hold the reins. Like this. Here we go."

A light touch to the mule's flanks was all it took. Gabe knew he and the other people weren't the only ones glad to be going back to the settlement in the bottom of the canyon. All in all, he was feeling pretty satisfied until Holly spoke.

"Your radio and my gun are under all that fresh mud from the flash flood. One of the criminals we've been pursuing managed to slip by and start up the trail. I made the mistake of asking him for help before I saw how he was dressed. That was when I realized he was one of the men in the Vegas footage."

It didn't take a lot of imagination to figure out what she was trying to say but he needed to be certain. "You're sure he was part of that cartel?"

"As sure as I can be until we get a crew in here to dig him out." She paused as if having trouble continuing.

"You tried to save him, regardless. I know you did."

There was a catch in her voice as she said, "Yes. I tried. He wouldn't listen." She sniffled. "I'm just thankful he didn't force us all to stay in the bottom of that gorge with him."

Gabe felt suddenly breathless. He nodded, stalling for time to regain his self-control before he sighed and said, "Yeah. Me, too."

SIX

As the adrenaline drained out of Holly's nervous system, she began to grow so weary she had to admit she probably couldn't have walked all the way back. Not without a good nap halfway there. The steady gait of the mule helped lull her, too.

Renee, however, had yet to come down from the high caused by their harrowing morning. "How can you guys be so matter-of-fact about it? I mean, I'm still shaking and you two are making silly jokes."

"I'm sorry if we offended you," Holly said. "We have to try to lighten up as soon as possible to stay sane. It's a coping mechanism. Rescuers and law enforcement officers do it because it works. Most of the time."

"What happens when it doesn't?" the other woman asked.

"You join the FBI," Holly said. If she hadn't been bone tired she might not have revealed so much. Now that she had, however, she saw no reason to stop explaining. "I was considering becoming a park ranger, like McClellan, here. I even spent a summer as a volunteer right here in the Grand Canyon."

"Why did you change your mind? Too hard?"

Holly snorted a wry chuckle. "The job isn't easy, particularly for the Search and Rescue teams and law enforcement rangers. But that's not why I applied to the FBI instead."

Thoughts and memories of losing Ivy covered her like a heavy wool blanket, weighing her down, body and soul. "It was because of my baby sister," Holly explained. "After she was kidnapped and murdered, all I wanted to do was help catch whoever had done it. During the course of that investigation I met lots of detectives, and it was the FBI that most impressed me."

She saw Gabe's shoulders square. He didn't turn to look at her but that didn't matter. He'd taken it all in. She knew he had. Was he going to comment? Waiting, she heard nothing from any of her companions. That was just as well because the morning's stress had weakened her tight hold on her emotions and she was afraid she'd cry if she had to talk about her sister much more.

The mule had made good time and they were within sight of Spirit Station when Gabe broke the silence. He merely said "I'm sorry, Holly" before using his radio to report their position and request a status report.

That hadn't been a fluke, she realized. He had expressed empathy while saving her from having to reply. Not many people were that sensitive to the feelings of others, nor did they go out of their way to offer comfort. Oh, it happened. Of course it did. But this man, this senior ranger, wasn't usually that tender when it came to disappointments. He'd always seemed to be the kind who expected others to power through, and get on with life no matter what.

And she had, in her own way, when she'd aced the courses at Quantico. Cities were her normal focus but she'd proved she could adapt to just about anything when this manhunt had led her back to Grand Canyon National Park.

It didn't escape her notice that circumstances had also plunked her down in the territory patrolled by the extraordinary man who was in the process of rescuing her.

"Physically, not psychologically," Holly muttered. She might have been knee-deep in mud in that rift and needed help getting out, but the rest of her life was laid out just the way she wanted it. Period.

There was a welcoming committee of rangers waiting when Gabe delivered his muddy cargo. He handed the boy to Broadstreet and helped the mother into Hough's care. "Check them over. If there's nothing that needs immediate attention, we'll hold off on an evac until things settle down."

Each man agreed and they escorted their patients out of sight and out of danger. Holly made a less-than-graceful exit over the mule's rump and fortunately did not received a swift kick for her daring.

"Nice dismount, Forbes. Do they teach that technique in FBI classes?"

"Nope. That was strictly ad-lib." She grinned. "I'm glad my legs held me up when I hit the ground. That is one big mule."

"Ah, right," Gabe teased. "You're a city girl."

"Hey! I know enough to handle myself out here," she insisted.

Gabe shrugged. "Maybe. And maybe you know just enough to get yourself into big trouble." He sobered. "You could have been killed in the flash flood. You know that, right?"

"I climbed instead of trying to outrun it, didn't I?"

"That you did."

Stretching and flexing like a dancer preparing to perform, Holly yawned. "Man, I'm beat. Dodging gunmen and floating boulders really takes a lot out of a person." She smiled at the now-placid mule that had carried them all so ably. "So does bouncing up and down on his rear end."

"Picky, picky, picky. If I'd commandeered a horse, you'd probably have had to walk. They aren't built for hauling heavy loads the way my long-eared friend is."

"Then it's a good thing I've missed a few meals lately."

"Hungry? Energy bars suit you?"

"Do you have any chocolate-flavored ones?"

Gabe rolled his eyes and shook his head, then began rooting through a nearby pack. "Didn't you bring anything to eat?"

"Apparently it slipped my mind. I mean, this isn't the wilderness. I know they sell food at the rim."

"Spirit Ranch has a dining room, too, but it's just for guests. They have to pack in everything they serve so they're pretty stingy with it." He offered her a choice of several energy bars. "We have a kitchen and storage pantry at the ranger station, of course, but I don't recommend you knock on their door and ask for food right now."

"What's the latest on that situation?" Holly asked.

He noted that she was concentrating on opening her energy bar rather than looking him in the eye. That was understandable, particularly since her decision to go off on her own had taken him away from his regular duties. He wasn't faulting her but didn't doubt she was feeling guilty.

"We're on hold, waiting for the negotiator to arrive." He arched a brow. "Yes, it's driving me up the wall, in case you were wondering."

"Figures. I'm pretty antsy, too." Saluting by raising her snack to him, she said, "Thanks. I don't know if I'd have insisted on responding to the shouts I heard if I hadn't been so primed to do something. Anything. I am sorry for causing you extra concern."

Gabe huffed. "That's one way to put it." He took two steps closer and lightly touched her shoulder. "I've been in a lot of tough spots since I became a park ranger but I can't recall ever being quite as scared as I was today when I learned about the flash flooding. And I didn't even know you were mixed up with a crook at the time. When you get yourself into trouble, you do a bang-up job of it."

She chewed and swallowed, then said, "I always try to outperform civilians. It impresses them."

"Yeah, well, you got my attention, too. But from now on, no side trips or no going off alone. I made the mistake of not stopping you before. I won't make the same mistake again."

Holly arched her eyebrows and tilted her head to one side while studying him. "In case you're confused about this, McClellan, I don't take orders from you."

When he opened his mouth to speak she waved him to silence.

"Hold on. I'm not trying to take over this operation or tell you what to do. I'm just saying that I intend to look out for the interests of the FBI and do my job. As long as my goals mesh with yours, we won't have any conflicts."

"You think not?" He unscrewed the top on a fresh bottle of water and drank. "Seems to me you could have used my backup when that guy took your gun and radio."

"He was armed to start with," Holly said. "I wasn't about to try to shoot him when he was aiming at the child."

"Perfectly sensible."

"Thank you."

"I wonder if he was the one who shot at us before. I don't suppose he told you how he managed to slip away or how many men are left at our station."

"Unfortunately, no. He was alone on the trail and headed up so I assumed he was a hiker. That's why I didn't suspect him at first. If I'd been able to see his clothing before I asked for his help, I might have figured out who he was sooner and been better prepared."

"Maybe we should require all criminals to rattle like a diamondback before they strike. Might cut down on crime."

She made a silly face at him. "Very funny."

"I thought so." Gabe shrugged and drank more water. He had to keep their conversations as light as possible because every time he allowed himself to picture her being swept away by the flash flood, it tied him in knots. He'd tried to tell himself he felt the same about the loss of any life and quickly realized that wasn't true. He was sorry for the drowned crook, sure, and would have been even more upset to lose tourists, but that wasn't the same as what he was feeling in regard to Holly Forbes. He admired her beyond reason. Why he did was the critical question for which he currently had no answer.

Another thing Gabe refused to contemplate was what it would be like to bid her goodbye once this rescue and capture was over. The FBI was bound to send her away. Seeing each other again or having a chance to get well acquainted was not likely.

Thinking about that possibility was more than ridiculous, Gabe told himself. Forming a personal relationship would mean a total change of lifestyle for one or both of them and he was perfectly happy right where he was. He'd met and exceeded his goals and had no intention of ever being anything but a National Park Ranger.

"So get your head on straight and stop dreaming of a different future," he told himself in disgust. "You worked too hard to get where you are to even consider throwing it all away for a pretty face."

Except Agent Holly Forbes was so much more than that, his mind countered. She was courageous, intelligent, clever and more fun to match wits with than anyone he'd ever known. Given other circumstances he might have let himself fall for her.

His radio crackled. The negotiator had arrived at Lee's Ferry and was being brought down to their location by boat because that was the fastest way.

Gabe's eyes met Holly's and saw a query there. "Our negotiator is on his way."

"It's a man, then?"

"Yes."

"Where will he come ashore?"

"Over there. It's not an official landing area but allowed in this case. Why?"

"Because I intend to be there to greet him," she said flatly, "and ask why they decided to go over my head when I'm also trained to negotiate."

"Maybe they figured men would respond best to other men." The scowl she gave him left nothing to the imagination. She was furious.

"Men. They always assume a woman is less capable."

Gabe decided to speak his mind. "Sometimes they are."

"Oh, terrific. You, too?"

"Hear me out," Gabe urged, lightly taking her arm to discourage her from storming off. "We're generally stronger and larger, for one thing. And we tend to keep our emotions under control better than women do." He arched an eyebrow and gave her a quirky grin. "Like now."

She jerked her arm away but didn't leave. "Point taken."

"However," he went on, "in the case of dealing with scared kids or being a crack shot or even having equal or more stamina, a woman can excel."

Seeing her shoulders begin to relax told him he was on the right track. "You managed to rescue that woman and her son despite having little gear and no recent training here in the park. I consider that exemplary. Even if the higher-ups at the Bureau don't fully appreciate you, I do."

Holly's wide eyes misted, reflecting the towering rocks in the distance and the sky above. Gabe didn't tease her about being too emotional. He was pleased to have had the chance to offer moral support, especially considering what she'd revealed about losing her sister. If she hadn't experienced such a dramatic event, perhaps she might even have become a ranger the way she'd once intended.

But she hadn't. She wasn't. And imagining working beside her all the time was idiotic. While she was here in the canyon, he'd look after her. Once she left, he'd put her out of his mind the way he had other women, other friends who came and went because they didn't fit his lifestyle.

For the first time in recent memory, Gabe realized— and admitted—he was lonely.

SEVEN

Portions of the Colorado River were turbulent as it wended through the canyon. The wider area at Spirit Station was placid compared to the rapids. Just to the west of the settlement, two footbridges—Kaibab and Bright Angel—connected the North and South Kaibab Trails where Bright Angel Creek fed into the impressive river.

Holly stood in the center of the first bridge with Gabe, watching for the approach of the FBI agent's raft. When she spotted a large one being manned by a crew of fit young men she asked, "Is that what we're waiting for?"

"Yes. I recognize some of my rangers. They're dressed as tourists but it's them."

"Good," she said. "More muscle."

She watched his expression until she saw him realize she was baiting him about male superiority. Then his eyes narrowed and he gave her a mock scowl. "Right."

Holly laughed. "Took you long enough. I was beginning to wonder if you were paying attention."

"I have a lot on my mind."

Sobering, she touched his forearm. "I know. Sorry. What's the plan now?"

"We hold our observation positions and keep our fingers crossed."

"A little praying probably wouldn't hurt, either," she offered.

"Absolutely. I just wish we knew how the injured ranger inside is doing and how many civilians are being held."

"I suppose you've tried phoning and asking?"

When Gabe nodded, she was relieved he hadn't taken her question as criticism. She knew he was good at his job. She'd seen plenty of examples in the past and he was even more impressive now. The problem for her was rooted in the psychological differences in the way men and women reasoned. Males tended to be linear thinkers while her mind bounced all over the place when she let it. That wasn't necessarily a bad thing. It sometimes produced ideas that were actually useful. Offbeat, maybe, but good nevertheless. That was one of the oddities that had not been on Gabe's list of female assets. Before she left the canyon, she was going to make sure he understood how valuable her input could be.

The raft carrying the negotiator beached upriver about a hundred yards and began to offload passengers and cargo. Holly kept up with Gabe as he jogged to meet it and introduced himself.

The moment she recognized the older man the Bureau had sent, she gritted her teeth. Andrew "I Am Always Right" Summers. Terrific. She might as well go sit in the shade and eat another energy bar. That man was never going to listen to a thing she said. Gabe would have a better chance of being heard but even he was going to be surprised once Agent Summers started issuing orders as if he were the only voice of reason.

Squat, perspiring and looking uncomfortable in his

khaki clothing and fabric hat with sun flaps, Summers awkwardly disembarked with help from the fit and agile rangers. He shook Gabe's hand. "I was briefed on the way in, McClellan. Take me to your command post and then show me the closest vantage point. I'll work from there."

If Gabe was put off, he gave no indication of it. Holly fell into step behind the men. Talk about feeling like a third wheel. She might as well be invisible. Then again, maybe that wasn't so bad. At least she'd escaped notice by Summers. Best to be thankful.

Pausing at the open-sided tent denoting his temporary command post, Gabe dispersed the relief crew to personally notify the others that help had arrived.

"Isn't that the hard way?" Summers asked.

"We're keeping radio communication to a minimum," Gabe replied.

"That's about to end."

"I beg your pardon?"

Holly knew what was coming and wondered how her calm, self-controlled ranger friend was going to react. His opinion might not show but she was sure she'd be able to tell what he was really thinking.

"I'm going to need a good phone connection," Summers said flatly.

"There are no telephone lines down here," Gabe said.

The older man rolled his eyes. "Cell phones, man. Satellite. This is the twenty-first century."

"No cell service, Agent Summers." Holly saw Gabe stifle a smile as he continued. "The canyon is too deep and the angle is wrong."

"Radios, then. Give me yours. And have somebody fetch my megaphone."

Gabe stepped away far enough to use his radio without letting the agent grab it. Using the usual frequency, he ordered several of his rangers to bring the gear from the landing, then told them to take a *vacation*.

Covering her mouth, Holly smothered a chuckle. The astonished look on the other FBI agent's face was priceless.

Summers held out a hand. "Radio, please."

"I'll get you one in a few minutes. This is mine." Stepping out, he gestured. "Follow me. You, too, Agent Forbes."

"Who?"

"Agent Holly Forbes. She's been on this case since it began over in Vegas. Surely, you were informed."

Summers waved a hand toward her. "Heard something about it."

"Good, because she's a valued advisor here in the park."

Holly could have jumped for joy, thrown her arms around Gabe's neck and kissed him. She did nothing of the kind, of course, except in her mind. That was enough to redden and warm her cheeks, particularly when Gabe caught her eye and winked.

She mouthed a silent thank-you and received a polite nod in return. If he'd been wearing his full uniform, she was sure he'd have tipped his Smoky Bear–style hat to her.

Bottom line, she reminded herself, they were all there to do the same job. That meant getting along. It also meant letting Summers do the talking, and praying he'd have success liberating the hostages and saving lives. She didn't have to like him to respect his skills.

God willing, he'd help them accomplish their mutual goals before anyone else died. Having been shot at twice and almost smothered in mud and debris, she was more than ready to embrace an end to this standoff.

* * *

Seven of Gabe's men had erected a makeshift barricade that faced the front of Spirit Station. Behind the station building was a rockfall with boulders the size of cars. Rubble along the sides precluded a clear passage to the river unless a person was skilled at scaling unstable rocks. That helped Gabe more than it did the criminals because he could concentrate most of his manpower along the most accessible side.

If he had known the type of man the FBI was sending, he would still have set up their barriers the way he had, but he might have moved the initial access point even farther away. It was a surprise that those nervous, twitchy crooks didn't fire at Summers the moment he spoke with that megaphone.

"Attention in the ranger station. This is Special Agent Summers of the FBI. You're surrounded. Put down your weapons. Come out with your hands up and no one will get hurt."

Nothing happened. Gabe had figured it wouldn't. He borrowed a spare radio from one of his men and passed it to the negotiator. "I think your first idea was better," Gabe said. "Here."

"About time."

Staying crouched behind the electric farm carts and bales of hay from the mule barn that were piled in a curved line, Gabe worked his way over to Holly. "What's with that guy?"

"Andrew has an overblown opinion of himself. I will say he's accumulated a pretty impressive success record but that's when he's dealing with real criminals. These guys are different. They're basically businessmen who got themselves into this mess by fronting the money to a gang for drugs, then running for their lives when the shooting started. I doubt they have the slightest idea how to get themselves out of trouble."

"Surely he was briefed about all that."

"If he listened. He tends to form an opinion quickly and hang on to it like a stubborn child with the last ice-cream cone."

"Interesting analogy. You must be hungry again."

"I hadn't thought about it but I could be."

He pretended to check his pockets. "Sorry. Fresh out of food. If you go back to the place we left the extra supplies, will you bring me a bottle of water and a snack, too? Please?"

"Sure. No problem since you asked nicely." She eyed the back of the negotiator. "I'll even bring something for him."

Gabe quirked a smile. "Well, okay. Just don't overdo it."

"Not a chance." She returned his grin. "Be careful and keep your head down while I'm gone, will you? No heroics."

Gabe chuckled softly. "Absolutely. I can't act like a hero again anyway. I gave back my trusty steed."

"The mule?"

"Hey, a steed is a steed. Don't knock the ones with long ears. They can outdo a horse, especially in country like this."

"Same as you and your men are far better suited to this operation than our negotiator," Holly remarked, squinting at the man's back. "We'll need to keep a close eye on him."

"We?" Gabe felt his grin widening when he noted her reddened cheeks.

"Yes, *we*, Mr. Ranger, and don't you forget it."

He laughed aloud. "Never."

EIGHT

There was enough activity in the valley to keep Holly from feeling complacent. Not only were the newly arrived rangers in plain clothes mingling and issuing warnings, there were enough tourists present to create confusion.

Men mounted on mules stood as sentries, keeping the outsiders at bay and isolating the rescue attempt, but the rest of the valley reminded her of what an anthill looked like after being stepped on. There didn't seem to be a lot of purposeful direction to many of the hikers and tourists and even the red-shirted staff members of Spirit Ranch were acting frazzled. That figured. After all, their livelihoods depended upon keeping their visitors happy, and being under siege wasn't exactly conducive to serenity.

Holly headed straight for the cache of supplies. A good-looking man with a crew cut and muscled, well-tanned arms was standing guard while several other men were working on a nondescript gray private raft in the background. "Can I help you?" the guard asked.

Holly had lost her official ID in the flash flood so she bluffed through. "Agent Forbes, FBI. Ranger McClellan sent me for water and snacks. He's part of the team set up over by the station."

"He sent you? Why?"

This was the perfect time to play up her femininity so she bit the bullet and resorted to doing it. "I'm the least important member of the crew right now and he can spare me," she said, sounding every bit as disgruntled as she was starting to feel.

"That so?"

"Yes." She gritted her teeth. "That's so."

The man grinned. "You think you can carry what you need or do you want help?"

"I'm stronger than I look," she said, stepping forward until he moved out of her way.

"Whatever you say, ma'am."

"You can call me Agent Forbes, or just Agent."

He gave a mock salute. "Yes, ma'am, Agent Forbes. Pleasure to make your acquaintance. You can call me Bodie."

Looking him up and down, assessing him, Holly managed a lopsided smile. "I suppose Bodie is one of the names I can call you if you refuse to drop the *ma'am*."

He laughed. "I'm sorry. I truly am, but it's a habit. My mama would have taken a switch to me if I hadn't called every lady 'ma'am' when I was growin' up in Georgia."

Holly sighed. "Sorry if I sounded cross. I worked very hard to become an agent."

"I get it," Bodie said. He started helping her load a pack. "All law enforcement tends to favor men. I'm not sayin' that's right. It's just how it is. Better now than back when my daddy was a cop, though."

"Women have to be at the top of their class in order to succeed." Holly wondered if he was going to argue with her.

Instead, he laughed again. "Yes, ma...sir."

She was still grinning widely as she bade the young ranger goodbye and shouldered the pack. She had worked hard. Very hard. And she still did, every day. Her job meant the world to her, as it should. Every criminal, every killer, she put behind bars was one less on the street to threaten helpless citizens like Ivy. Her younger sister had been on the brink of adulthood, ready for the adventures life brought, about to start college and begin her studies to become a doctor. Until someone had beaten her to death for no reason.

A shiver skittered along Holly's spine, causing her to look back. Bodie waved casually. But behind him, by the beached gray raft, two surly-looking workers were staring back at her. They didn't look like part of the crew who had ferried the last group of rangers. Still, they'd need a permit to enter the canyon so there should be no reason for her to be uneasy. Yet she was.

Despite the heat bouncing off the steep rock walls and warming the valley, Holly felt chilly. She quickened her pace. She was trained. Ready for anything. So why was the urge to hurry back to Gabe so strong? Perhaps it was because he'd rescued her so recently. Or maybe she was subconsciously recalling the past when he'd helped other summer volunteers pull her out of the river when she'd tried to make a solo rescue without a safety rope. Whatever the reason, her desire to be back with the rangers was almost a compulsion, particularly when it came to Gabe.

Thinking of him, picturing him, brought a little relief. He was special, more than a former role model. He was an extraordinary man who treated her as an equal, not because he was required to do so but because he truly believed it. In her eyes, that made him a superhero.

* * *

Gabe saw Holly returning because he'd been apprehensively waiting for her. Rational thought kept being pushed aside by his desire to know she was safe. To see for himself that nothing had happened to harm her.

"It's normal to worry about my men," he muttered, knowing that was stretching the truth in more ways than one. Holly wasn't a genuine part of his crew and she certainly wasn't a man. Oh, he'd treat her like one of the guys. That was a given. But his heart was convinced he would never be able to view her that way in his private thoughts.

"Which won't be a problem after today or tomorrow," he said, wondering why that conclusion bothered him.

She was close enough to overhear. Smiling, she asked, "What won't be a problem?"

Gabe recovered and gestured over his shoulder. "Your FBI buddy. If you hadn't vouched for him, I'd think he was an imposter instead of a seasoned negotiator. Doesn't he do anything except deliver ultimatums?"

"If I remember correctly, he'll change tactics later. Right now he's testing their responses to authority."

Ushering her closer and helping her drop the pack, Gabe made sure she was hidden from view. "He should be glad I'm not on the receiving end of his threats. If I were those guys in the station, I'd probably take a potshot at him."

"I imagine he's wearing a vest."

Gabe huffed. "Not on his head."

"I don't think they make a big enough bulletproof hat for Andrew's head. But he is good at ducking."

"Apparently. He's lived this long."

Chuckling, Holly merely rolled her eyes. Dark humor

was so much a part of both their jobs, it was natural to fall
back on it when the going got tough. That was another
thing Gabe appreciated about her. She shared the ten-
dency to use sarcasm and supposedly inappropriate comments as an emotional release instead of acting surprised
or offended. Basically, she got him. And he understood
her, too. That hadn't been as evident when they'd originally met and gotten acquainted but it was certainly clear
now. It was a relief to be able to be himself around her.

Was that why he was so attracted to the pretty FBI
agent? he wondered. Maybe. The list of things about her
that he liked and admired was growing by the minute,
which was disconcerting to say the least.

Gabe cleared his throat. "What's your feeling about
the atmosphere out there? Are we handling things okay
or are the tourists about to mutiny?"

"A little of both." Holly handed him a bottle of cold
water. "Some supplies are starting to run low because
we're keeping everybody together down here but so far,
so good. As long as they stay hydrated they'll be okay.
Maybe not thrilled but healthy. Beyond that, I wouldn't
worry about civilians. They'll muddle through."

"I suppose rumors are flying."

"Mostly true ones from what I could overhear. They've
figured out we have a serious problem and are basically
trying to get shots with cameras and cell phones to send
home to friends. Your guys are holding the line okay."

"So they've reported. I just wanted your opinion."

Holly beamed at him. "That's what I love about you,
McClellan. You actually do want to hear what I think.
Lots of people ask and then don't listen."

He tilted his chin to point. "Like Agent Summers?"

"Oh, yeah. He's the poster boy for Misogynists-R-Us."

"His age probably has something to do with that."

"I think he was asleep during the last fifty or sixty years. He hasn't changed with the times." Holly sighed. "He's not the only agent I've met who thinks I'm just eye candy rather than actually being qualified."

Gabe almost choked on his water when he started to laugh in the middle of a swallow. "*Eye candy?* Now who's stuck in the past?"

Holly laughed with him and slapped him on the back to stop his coughing. "Sorry."

"I'll live." As he'd been talking to her, he'd also kept part of his attention on the chillingly quiet ranger station. Now he set aside his water bottle and raised binoculars. "Uh-oh."

She was at his side, eager for a peek. "What? What do you see?"

"I'm not sure." Gabe handed the binoculars to her and waited while she adjusted them to her vision. "Look toward the rear. In that pile of big boulders that sits to the east? I thought I saw movement."

"I...don't... Maybe. It's really hard to tell with the rising heat making the air shimmer. Could it have been a mirage?"

"I suppose." Knowing she was probably right wasn't enough for him. Not this time. "Keep watching. I'm going to work my way around to a different vantage point."

"I'll go with you."

"No." The set of her jaw and sparks in her eyes didn't make him change his mind. "I need a steady observer to keep an eye on me and keep looking for whatever I saw, assuming I didn't imagine it."

"But..."

He could tell that his logic was getting through to her.

"I mean it, Holly. I'll have a radio with me, muted. Don't try to contact me. If I need help, I'll call for it. In the meantime, I don't want any chatter to tip off those guys holding out in the station. As far as they know, we'll all be sitting here waiting for Agent Summers to talk them into surrendering."

"All but you."

"Hey, I could send one of my crew but the medics are crucial and so are law enforcement." As he spoke he was stripping off his utility belt and uniform shirt, leaving only his khaki cargo shorts and a T-shirt. Then he grabbed a forest green ball cap and put it on backward to hide the National Park Service logo. "How do I look?"

"Like a ranger in a poor disguise," she said wryly. "You're too clean for a hiker and too dry for a river rat."

"Hiking all the way around the building should fix that," Gabe replied. "I'll brief my rangers before I leave and borrow a radio. You can keep mine." He managed a smile for her benefit. "You're staying put, right? Promise?"

Although she shrugged and made a face, she nodded. "Promise. Anything else?"

He sobered, knowing it would kill the mood but needing moral support. "Yes," he said. "While you're at it, you might want to pray for all of us."

"Redundant but sensible," Holly said. "I haven't stopped talking to God since my partner was wounded in Vegas." Reaching out, she touched his arm.

A shiver ran through Gabe despite the hot day. He saw Holly's eyes widen at the same time his own jaw dropped slightly. She'd felt it, too. He knew she had.

It's because of the tension and this untenable situation, he told himself, *nothing more.*

He stepped back. Broke contact. Yearned to at least give her a parting hug. That was crazy. She'd laugh in his face if she didn't slap it.

Therefore, he reasoned, turning away to brief his team before heading for the ranger station, *kissing her is totally out of the question.*

When he realized what his mind had just suggested, he blushed. Tried to refocus. Checked the position of the pistol now tucked at the small of his back under the hem of his T-shirt, then tugged down the shirt and started on his mission.

Birds called overhead and swallows swooped. A squirrel chattered. Groups of antsy tourists seemed to notice him despite his so-called disguise and several tried to approach but he was moving too fast.

Away from Holly. Toward possible danger.

And still he imagined kissing her.

NINE

Holly'd had a bothersome flaw in her personality for as long as she could remember. She hated to wait. For anything or anybody. That was one of the mistakes she'd made that had gotten Ivy in trouble. Holly had gone to pick her up after an evening class, as promised and had waited what she considered a reasonable amount of time. Then, after texting and getting no reply, she'd driven away, assuming Ivy had gone out with friends and was simply being inconsiderate. It had happened more than once before.

Exactly what had occurred after that hadn't been proved but the authorities suspected the younger woman had been waiting for a taxi when she was picked up by someone else, beaten to death and dumped by the side of the road.

Hardly a day went by that Holly didn't relive the guilt and wish she'd had the patience to wait just a little longer. Which was why she was currently pacing behind the makeshift barricade and paraphrasing to herself about "letting patience have its perfect work," as scripture taught.

She huffed. "Yeah, patience. Big whoopee. Like I've ever had as much as I need." Knowing that truth and dealing with the repercussions were at war in her mind. She'd managed to do well on her field testing for the Bureau by sheer force of will, but there were times in real life when she felt as if she'd jump out of her skin if she didn't act. Do something. Anything. This was one of those times.

Most of the rangers with her, including Gabe, had changed to cooler cargo shorts and were taking turns observing the station while Andrew Summers continued to broadcast into the void. When he switched to using the handheld radio, Holly thought her stomach was going to give back that last bottle of water. Hands fisted, she listened.

"Attention in the ranger station," Summers said firmly. "I know you can hear me. It's my job to help you work this out so nobody gets hurt. I don't want to send armed men in there but I will if I have to."

The radio crackled with muttered cursing.

"No reason for that attitude," Summers said. "Calm down and let's discuss this. I'm willing to be reasonable."

Holly was not surprised that there was no answer from the men in the station. Any change in tactics would set the crooks' nerves on edge, and threatening an armed attack was bound to put them on guard even more. They would check windows. Scan their surroundings. And if they did that, they could spot Gabe approaching.

Worse, he'd muted his own radio so he wouldn't know what Summers had said. She couldn't warn him. If ever there was a good reason to break protocol and follow the courageous ranger, this was it.

"Patience, Holly, patience," she told herself, countering urges to move with reasons to obey Gabe's orders.

A brief scan of the rocks behind the station showed nobody. That proved nothing. Just because she couldn't see danger lurking in the shadows, it didn't mean it wasn't there. Suppose one of those shady men down by the river was involved. Yes, it was unlikely. Unfortunately, she'd neglected to mention her intuitive reaction to Gabe.

Her hand went to her waist and rested on her empty holster. Limited in firepower by her earlier encounter with one of the fugitives meant she now carried only her holdout gun. She pulled the small revolver from its holster, flipped open the loaded cylinder and peered down the short barrel from the rear before closing it. It looked clean. Which meant she wasn't exactly helpless.

"Okay, so now what?" she wondered aloud.

None of the rangers were close enough to hear and answer. Holly scanned the group. Most were kicking back, saving energy for whatever was to come. *As they should be*, she thought.

Binoculars brought the faraway rock field into clearer focus. Where was Gabe? And what about the felon he thought he'd seen trying to sneak off? She doubted a seasoned ranger would have imagined an enemy where there was none, yet at this moment she was seeing only rocks.

Holly stiffened, grasping the binoculars tighter. What, or who, was *that*? It certainly wasn't an adult and unless she was imagining things, there was more than one small person at the edge of the rockfall. What were kids doing playing around out there? Where were their parents?

She shivered at the thought of innocent children caught in the midst of an ambush, and at the mental image of Gabe letting down his guard enough to be harmed because of it. That was not going to happen to him—or to those kids. Not on her watch.

Holly started forward, intending to alert one of the rangers and beg him to do something. Contrary reasoning stopped her. Once she notified the others, they would be bound by duty to force her to stay away. Chances were they wouldn't break the rules and intervene without a direct order, either. She had to handle this situation herself. Foolish or not, there was no other way.

No one stopped her or even seemed to notice as she left the barricade. Small of stature and a woman, she was practically invisible to most officers and to a large segment of the civilian population. In this case that was definitely to her advantage.

What was her plan? she asked herself, realizing she had none other than to reach those errant children and pull them back, out of danger. That was enough. She was a quick thinker. A seasoned adversary. She could make further choices once she was closer and could see exactly what she faced.

And, hopefully, she could also keep Gabe from being targeted. That was her main goal.

That and staying alive.

As Gabe worked his way through the sparse, low brush and between the scrubby tamarisk and willow trees of the canyon floor, he encountered several tourists trying to take pictures of the besieged ranger station. One man was so engrossed in getting the perfect shot, he didn't notice Gabe coming up behind him. A firm hand on the tourist's shoulder got his attention. The guy jumped and yelped like a coyote with its paw stuck in a trap.

"Whoa, man, you scared me. Don't sneak up on a guy like that."

Gabe glared. "You know this area is off-limits, right?"

"Yeah, yeah. Stuffy rangers tried to stop me but I

outfoxed them and cut around. If I can get the pics I want, I can sell them for enough to pay for my vacay."

"And endanger other lives in the process. Or don't you care?"

"I care. I care. I'm not hurtin' anything. I'm just standin' here, waiting for something interesting to happen. No crime in that."

Gabe reached into his pocket and produced his badge. "Disobeying a park ranger here is the same as doing it to the police in a city. We're law enforcement. And we take our jobs very seriously."

The sight of the badge seemed to knock the wind out of the trespasser. He gave a weak smile and shrugged. "Okay. Sorry. Um, can I go now?"

"As long as you go back behind the lines we've set up. And stay there. This isn't a game. I know you came here to enjoy yourself but it won't be at someone else's expense. Got that?"

"Yes, sir. Understood."

Gabe paused barely long enough to watch the interloper jog back the way he'd come, then continued his mission. One of the hardest things for rangers to get across to park visitors was their authority. They were supposed to keep the peace without looking as if they were doing it. In other words, make the public feel welcome and safe, yet keep them out of trouble.

Gabe huffed. It would be a lot easier if they'd obey the simple rules that were meant for their own good, such as staying on the trails and not climbing railings to peer over the edge into the mile-deep abyss. Most of them got away with it. Some didn't. During peak summer months, his Search and Rescue crews averaged at least two critical patients or accidental deaths a day and sometimes more. If a slip and fall didn't cause the problem, simple dehydration could bring hallucinations and lead to a coma, particularly if the victim was hiking without proper preparation.

The ranger station lay ahead to his right. Gabe concentrated on working his way around it at a distance. There were enough scrubby trees to mask his approach and, thanks to subdued colors of his clothing, he felt well hidden.

A joyful-sounding squeal split the air. Gabe froze. Hair at the nape of his neck and on his forearms stood up. The noise was coming from behind the building. Of all the sounds he might expect to hear, high-pitched laughter was the least likely, yet that was exactly what it was.

Moving in a crouch, he worked his way from tree to tree, taking care to keep an eye on the windows and door of the station. Blinds had been pulled, which was to his advantage—as long as nobody inside decided to take a peek.

More laughing and screeching echoed. *Kids?* He clenched his jaw. Was that what he'd seen in the first place?

Well, it didn't matter. If one of the killers was trying to escape, it was Gabe's job to stop him. If some kids had managed to sneak past other rangers and had entered dangerous territory, taking care of them was his job, too. And after he'd rescued the children he suspected were playing in the rocks, he'd have a serious talk with their parents.

That was assuming he could get to them without being spotted and was able to shepherd them out of danger before the criminals holding the station figured out what was going on.

"Yeah. No sweat." Gabe shook his head in disgust. "Just when I thought we had the problem contained."

Making a dash for the nearest corner of the stone-and-wood building, he flattened himself against the wall, breathing hard and trying to keep from making gasping noises.

He waited. Nothing happened. Nobody moved inside that he could tell and the sound from among the boulders had ceased.

Slowly, cautiously, he drew his gun, his thumb on the safety, index finger resting against the trigger guard. Then he held his breath and leaned just far enough to peek around the corner. What he saw across the expanse of rough, boulder-strewn terrain took his breath away.

Incredulous, he tamped down the urge to shout. There were children, all right. Two young boys. And holding their hands on the opposite side of the station yard was a familiar woman.

Unbelievable. Holly Forbes was right in the midst of the danger despite his firm orders to stay put.

There was no way he could reach her without exposing himself to being shot at so he held his position. And seethed. Wondered if he had ever been this angry with anybody else.

Gabe was beyond words. If Holly had been standing in front of him right then, ready to take an official dressing-down, he wouldn't have known where to start.

A slight noise inside the station building caught his attention. He raised his gun and pivoted around the corner.

Holly's gaze met his. She drew the children closer and froze, apparently waiting for him to recognize her.

Gabe gestured with a flick of the gun barrel.

Holly nodded and started away, tugging the boys with her.

The rear door creaked open. A rifle poked out.

Gabe did the only thing he could. He shouted. "Drop the gun or I'll shoot!"

The long barrel jerked upward as a shot went wild.

In the milliseconds afterward, before the sound had died away, Gabe realized no one could have been hit because of the angle.

Nevertheless, his heart was about to pound out of his chest and his legs felt useless. He leaned hard against the building to pull himself together while he replayed the scene in his mind, insisting his assumptions had to be correct.

Still ready to fire if necessary, he reached for his radio and transmitted, "FBI, are you okay?"

Confused answers from others overlapped. Finally, Gabe heard the voice he was waiting for.

"That's affirmative," Holly radioed. "I have two children in custody and we're in the clear."

Gabe could hardly breathe. His pulse pounded in his ears and temples. Perspiration trickled into his eyes. He wiped them with his forearm, then rechecked the rocks for more people and concluded there was no one else there.

All the way back to the command post he muttered to himself about what had just happened while sending up prayers of thanks to God at the same time.

It was hard to be both thankful and furious. He kept trying to settle himself and failed. He had just renewed acquaintances with Holly and was ready to admit how special she was, yet the same traits that made her stand out were the ones that were driving him crazy.

She had brains, courage and the best of training. She

also schemed too much and acted as if she were a one-woman police force. Well, he couldn't have that. Not on his turf. And certainly not at the risk of her own life. It was time that somebody, namely him, reminded her she wasn't bulletproof.

One day, her bravado was going to get her into a situation she couldn't reason her way out of and he didn't want to see that happen.

The question was, how could he hope to exert enough influence to change her? To save her from herself? She was worth whatever it took to shake her up, even if it meant he had to cut loose and rant at her.

Right now, Gabe admitted, it was not going to be hard for him to abandon his usually calm persona and yell. Holly deserved it. And he didn't care if she hated him for it.

Any repercussions were worth enduring if his actions resulted in keeping her safe.

TEN

Both youngsters were crying by the time Holly dragged them behind the barricade. The taller of the two seemed less hysterical but he, too, was weeping softly.

Several rangers joined her, demanding to know what had happened.

"I spotted these kids playing in the rocks behind the station. Ranger McClellan had gone to check the opposite side so I figured it would be faster if I just ran over and brought them in myself."

One of the medics shook his head and rolled his eyes. "Boy, I'd hate to be you when Gabe gets back. What was the shooting about?"

"Somebody saw me but McClellan shouted and the shooter missed."

He eyed her from head to toe. "You have something against wearing a vest?"

Still elated by the successful rescue, Holly smiled. "Too hot and not stylish."

"I don't supposed you have anything important to report regarding conditions inside the station."

She shrugged. "I didn't stick around long enough to make an assessment. Sorry."

"Okay. I'll tell the other FBI agent. Between him and McClellan, you should be in for it good."

"Totally worth it," Holly replied.

Left alone for the moment, she crouched in front of the children. "All right, guys. What are your names?"

Choked sobs and sniffling were her answer.

"Have it your way. I'm Agent Forbes from the FBI." She was so relieved to have brought the children to safety, she wanted to smile again. Knowing better, she bit her lip and stayed solemn. "I'm going to call you Number One and Number Two."

The tearstained faces turned to look at each other, then back at Holly. The taller said, "FBI?"

"That's right."

"Where's your badge?" Two asked.

"That's a long story," Holly said. "The important thing is you were messing around where you didn't belong and you could have gotten hurt. What were you doing back there?"

"Looking for lizards."

"I see. Didn't you notice all the tape and the rangers?"

"We weren't hurtin' nothin'."

"Maybe not." Holly used her sternest expression and glared at them as she added, "But *you* could have been hurt." She concentrated on the younger boy. "What about you, Number One? Were you looking for lizards, too?"

He nodded rapidly. "Uh-huh."

"What about the rattlesnakes?"

Two sets of blue eyes widened. "The what?"

"Rattlesnakes. They're reptiles, too. If you can find lizards, you can find poisonous snakes in the same place."

One turned on Two. "It's Steve's fault. He made me."

"Shut up, Phillip. You'll get us in trouble."

Holly chuckled. "Okay. Steve and Phillip it is. So, guys, where are your parents?"

Phillip found the mud caked on the toes of his shoes fascinating. Steve answered for them both. "Taking naps in the shade." He gestured with his free hand. "Over there. See?"

"Do they have water with them? I want both of you to drink plenty. It was hot out there by those rocks."

Simultaneous nods pleased her. "Do I need to have a ranger walk you over there or can I trust you to go straight back to your mom and dad and stay with them?"

Steve took his younger brother's hand. "I'll watch him. It's my job."

"Then see that you do it better from now on," Holly warned. "Before you go, did you hear anything from inside the ranger station while you were there? Talking? Anything?"

"Nope."

"Okay." She spotted Gabe returning and decided to trust the children since she'd be able to watch them all the way. "Get going, guys. And no more messing around. You stay with your parents and do as they say. Got it?"

"Yes, ma'am."

She remembered correcting the young ranger, Bodie, for addressing her that way and smiled. Kids were different. Especially adorable ones like these boys. They'd clearly been raised to respect authority because neither of them had smart-mouthed her or argued. Good kids could still get into trouble. It was the nature of growing up. Of learning.

And speaking of learning, Holly took another look at Gabe and knew without a doubt that she was about to get a lecture from him. Judging by his expression and the fire in his eyes, it was not going to be an easy lesson, either.

If he'd dared grab her by the shoulders and give her a good shake, he might have. That was how upset he was. How scared he'd been when he'd seen the rifle barrel pointing in her direction.

Five more strides. Four. Three. He took a deep breath, fully intending to begin berating her, then opened his arms and embraced her instead. The hug wasn't planned; it just happened. And instead of pushing him away, she was returning the comforting gesture. Gabe took a deep breath and closed his eyes. A couple of tears trickled down his cheeks. Astonished, he just stood there, battling for self-control and feeling absolute relief from his toes to the top of his head.

The full breath released as a sigh. He felt her arms around his waist, her cheek laid on his chest, and it seemed like forever before he could make himself set her away.

Cupping her shoulders, he found his voice. "Why?"

"Because you were on the wrong side and it made sense for me to grab the kids." Holly met his gaze boldly.

Gabe eyed his men. "I can't believe they let you go."

"They didn't. I figured they'd try to keep me here if I told them what I was up to so I just went and did it."

A slow shake of his head gave him time to decide what else to say. Many of the thoughts whirling through his brain were unacceptable. Impossible to express without crossing a line. He finally settled on dark humor instead. "So, you're what they call TSTL."

"Is that a park ranger term?"

He huffed. "No. I think it started because of women in books and movies who walked into dark rooms unarmed when they already knew there were monsters hiding in the shadows."

"Ah."

Gabe watched light dawn in her eyes, saw her lips twitch in a lopsided grin as she said, "Too Stupid to Live?"

"That's the one."

"What I did wasn't stupid."

"It wasn't smart, either. You could have been killed."

"So could Steve and Phillip."

"You're on a first-name basis?"

"We are now." Holly pointed toward the family. "I think you should have a talk with the parents if you have time. Or send one of your rangers. They don't seem to realize how dangerous the canyon can be for children who aren't properly supervised."

"Now you're telling me how to do my job?" The relief he'd felt at being reunited with her was beginning to morph back into righteous anger. He'd lost friends, good men, because they hadn't followed protocol. Accidents were bad enough. Dying due to taking unnecessary chances was a total waste.

"No," Holly drawled. "I'm recommending that some lax parents be reminded of their responsibility to their innocent children." She pointed to one of the other rangers. "A warning would probably hold more weight coming from somebody in uniform, though. How about him? Or her?"

What galled Gabe the most was the fact that Holly was right on both counts. The visitors needed a lecture and a ranger in full uniform should be the one to deliver it. That was the trouble with that impossible FBI agent. She was right more often than she was wrong and he didn't like being on the receiving end of her so-called wisdom.

However, he also recognized how childish it would be for him to ignore her advice simply because of his ego. "Okay," Gabe said. "Wait here. I'll go get somebody to talk to them and you can go along to make the necessary introductions." When she opened her mouth to speak, he held up a hand like a cop stopping traffic. "No arguments. You chose to leave the post I'd assigned to you and go off on your own after promising to stay and keep watch. The way I see it, you owe me. And since you already know those kids, you're the perfect liaison."

Holly snapped a salute accompanied by a grin. "Yes, sir, Mr. Ranger. It will be a pleasure."

"That's not the last straw but you're close," he warned. "Being a ranger makes me proud. I'd rather you didn't make fun of it."

The way her face changed so rapidly told him all he needed to know even before she said, "I am sorry, Gabe. I didn't mean to belittle you. Not in the least. As a matter of fact, I look up to you."

Her earnestness softened his heart. "Apology accepted."

That brought back her smile. "Good. For a second there, I was afraid you were going to tease me about having to literally look up at you because I'm so short."

"I did think of it." He twitched at the corners of his mouth, wanting to mirror her silly grin. "But I was afraid you'd take offense."

"Not me, McClellan. I'm used to being the brunt of jokes."

"Maybe that's why you keep trying to prove you're better than everybody else."

Holly's hands fisted on her hips. "I do not."

"Do so." Gabe chuckled. "Every chance you get."

"Hmm…" She seemed to be pondering the possibility he was right. "Let's just say I have a lot to make up for."

"Might that have anything to do with the loss of your sister?" he asked wisely.

"Maybe. Probably. I told you that's why I joined the FBI in the first place but I didn't give you the details. It was my fault Ivy died."

"I doubt that."

"Well, don't," she insisted. "If I hadn't been so impatient, if I had waited for her, she'd have ridden home with me and she'd be alive." Holly's voice quavered, then grew strong again. "I was supposed to pick her up but she was late. I just assumed she'd gone off with friends again and left me sitting there because she was being inconsiderate."

"That wasn't the case?"

Holly shook her head and blinked back tears. "No. She'd been delayed after class. When she got to the parking lot late and I wasn't there, she tried to phone me. My ego kept me from answering right away and by the time I did, it was too late. I will never forgive myself for behaving that way."

"You were pretty young, too, weren't you?"

"Yes, but I was her big sister. I should have looked after her better." Holly glanced at the family she had reunited. "I hope little Steve took my warnings to heart."

Wanting to comfort her by refocusing her goals, Gabe took advantage of the situation. "Why don't you go make sure those people don't pack up and move? I'll send one of my rangers over ASAP to back you up. Every tourist we educate is hopefully one less who'll slip over the edge or fry their brains in the summer heat."

"Okay. I told the kids to drink lots of water but it

would be wise to check." She started to turn away, then paused. "Gabe?"

"Yes?"

"Thanks."

"For what?"

"For not looking at me the way my parents and friends did when I told them about driving away and leaving Ivy to fend for herself. That was the worst night of my life."

"It was a mistake," he countered. "You may have been upset with her but you weren't being malicious. If you had any inkling she'd be harmed, you'd have stayed. I know you would have."

"How can you be sure?"

Stepping closer he gently touched her shoulder for emphasis. "Because I know you. I see who you are, who you've become. Your character may not have been as polished back then but the basis for it existed. You've grown stronger because of what happened."

Holly blinked back tears and smiled. "And more opinionated?"

Nodding, he gazed at her, sensing a new connection. "Yes, that, too," Gabe said. "Nobody's perfect."

"In that case, here's another error you can add to my record. When I went to get our water and snacks, there were a couple of shady-looking characters down by the river and I forgot to tell you about them right away."

"Shady, how?"

"I don't know, exactly. It was just a feeling I got. Bad vibes. They stared at me. Gave me the creeps."

"It's probably nothing but I'll have that area checked out. Can you describe them?"

"Not well. They were cleaning out a raft and dressed as if they were tourists. When I noticed them, they were both bent over so I can't tell you how tall they were. Their hair was hidden under hats. One seemed a lot younger than the other. Sunburned, Caucasian. There was a disturbing aura about both of them."

"Like what? Sneaky? Guilty? Menacing?"

"Let me put it this way. If I saw either of them loitering on a dark street, I'd turn around and go the other way."

"That's good enough for me." Experience told him that the men were probably just moody because their river trip had been interrupted. Nevertheless, he did intend to have someone check IDs on all the young men waiting on the banks. There was an outside chance that the present situation was becoming more complicated than anyone realized. They'd already been surprised by the flood victim.

"You're not mad at me?" Holly asked.

"Furious," he joked, making sure she knew he wasn't serious by breaking into a grin. "Remember, intuition can be seriously overrated."

Expecting her to smile back at him, he was surprised when she raised an eyebrow instead. "We'll discuss that erroneous opinion after you've checked out the riverbank. I'm serious. I don't get this nervous for nothing."

"Wait a minute. Those guys bothered you that much and you didn't think it was necessary to share that information until now?"

Her brows arched. "That's the mistake. That's what I've been trying to explain."

"Not well." Sobering, he scanned the lengthening shadows as the sun dropped lower in the west. "Next time, don't beat around the bush, spit out the important parts first."

"I did."

"No, you didn't," Gabe said with a frown. "You tried to lead up to the main element by preparing me to accept it without blowing my stack. You did the same kind of thing when you were telling me about bringing in those kids. I don't need to hear reasons or excuses unless I ask for them. Just get to the point and let me decide how important your information is."

Although he was tempted to back off a little, he stuck to his declaration despite the dejection in Holly's expression. True, her need to please, to do things perfectly, had gotten her into the FBI and had earned her promotions. And as long as she stuck to analysis and figuring out puzzles by studying files, she'd be fine. What worried Gabe wasn't her intellect, it was her approach to danger. When a decision was hers alone, she acted quickly and decisively. However, if a problem required assistance or teamwork, she tended to skirt around it, waiting for clues from others to affirm her conclusions.

That often took long enough to place her in danger. If she learned one thing from him during this assignment, he was going to teach her to be straightforward. Someday, it could save her life.

ELEVEN

The long day had taken its toll on Holly. By nightfall, she, Agent Summers and the company of rangers were satisfied they had totally sealed off the station area and could permit park visitors to come and go on the corridor trails, South Kaibab, North Kaibab and Bright Angel. Although access to the two footbridges across the Colorado River was closely checked, tourists had been given permission to exit that way.

Spirit Ranch Lodge had provided whatever camping equipment the strike force had not packed in and had prepared a simple meal to be eaten at the scene. Shifts changed while men and women took needed rests. All except Gabe, Holly noted.

She approached him. "Aren't you tired?"

"Sure. Why?"

"Because you need to rest just like everybody else."

He was shaking his head as he said, "I'm not like everybody else."

"Yeah, I've noticed." She plunked down on a camp stool. "What makes you tick, McClellan? I mean, besides a huge hero complex."

His brow knit as he turned to her. "Is that what you really think or is it supposed to be a joke?"

"Um…" Holly raked her hair back with her fingers. "I'm not sure why I said that. Sorry if it offended you. I'm so tired I can hardly think straight."

"That I can understand." Yawning and stretching with his arms over his head, Gabe turned his gaze on her and held it steady. The extra attention made her shiver.

"You cold?"

"Not really. I'd forgotten how much the temps drop at night in the desert, though. It's probably really chilly up on the rim."

"Yeah."

Her hope that his thoughts had been diverted was quickly quashed when he asked, "So, what do you really think of me?"

The honest answer came too easily. "I think you're amazing."

"In what way?"

How could she explain without sounding like a lovestruck teenager? "Your devotion to duty, for starters. Not only do you make command decisions well, you stick to your mission."

"Better than you do, you mean?"

That made her blush. "Okay. I admit it. But we both have the welfare of others in mind."

"True." Gabe leaned forward, elbows resting on his knees, hands clasped between. "And in the case of the flash flooding, you made the right choices."

"Unlike what I did to my sister?" Holly's heart clenched. Gabe was judging her, too, now, just like all others. She supposed it was inevitable but it still hurt. A lot.

Reaching for her hand, he held it between both of his. "No, no. I wasn't even considering the long-ago past. What I meant was the way you ran into the line of fire to grab those kids today. That could have turned ugly in a heartbeat."

"I know. But I couldn't radio you to stand down and as soon as the guys barricaded in the station heard the kids laughing, they'd have been looking out the windows. They'd have spotted you for sure."

Gabe let go and rocked back. "Whoa. Don't try to blame your choice on me. I was doing fine. I didn't need any intervention."

"Yes, you did." She stood and put her hands on her hips. "You just didn't know it yet."

Facing her, sighing, Gabe rose, too. "Go get some rest, Agent Forbes. And stay behind our lines."

"That's an order?"

"Unofficially. I'd really like to be able to trust you to keep yourself safe."

"Of course you can trust me."

"Then prove it." He pointed to a small laptop. "I have work to do before this battery runs out of juice. I don't want to have to go beg the lodge to let me plug it in."

Holly just stood there, staring at his back as he turned away from her. With no internet available in the bottom of the canyon, she assumed he was working on scheduling or reading files he'd downloaded from a portable drive. It didn't really matter. Clearly, she had been dismissed.

Considering the way he had phrased his commands, she had no choice but to make herself scarce. Could she unwind enough to sleep? She doubted it. What she wanted was…

What *did* she want? The first thoughts that came to mind were not about work; they were about Gabe, which only served to prove his point. She needed to be more focused on the tasks at hand. On her job. On making sure her wounded FBI partner was avenged in a lawful way. Nothing else mattered. Nothing personal should ever be taken into account when she was on the trail of heinous criminals.

So what was wrong with her? It wasn't as if she had this problem of drifting concentration on a regular basis. Truth to tell, this was the first instance she could recall. The catalyst had to be her returning to the Grand Canyon and encountering that particular ranger again. Her unexpected reaction to him was very disconcerting. She was no kid. She was a responsible FBI agent with an exemplary record. No way was she going to let her emotions override logic.

Determined to talk herself out of being so enamored, Holly began to list priorities. One, she was on a lifelong mission of atonement. Two, she'd worked hard to attain her current status in the FBI.

And third? Her heart clenched as her mood plummeted. Marriage? Children? That wasn't meant to be for her. Her job was to look after other people's loved ones if they couldn't. To turn away from that goal was the same as deserting her sister all over again.

And she would never do that. Never.

Gabe walked the line of men keeping night watch behind the barricade, pausing when he came to the negotiator. "Did you take your break, Summers?"

His reply was curt. "As much as I needed."

"What's your assessment of the current status?"

"Dismal," the FBI man said with a grimace. "I've never run across such stubbornness. I can't decide if they're clueless or just idiots."

"According to Agent Forbes, they may be both."

"They've essentially stopped responding at all," Summers said. "I imagine they're even more worn-out than the rest of us are so I don't intend to let them sleep."

"No word on the wounded inside?"

He shook his head and polished his eyeglasses with the tail of his shirt. "None. We're considering calling in SWAT or army troops to storm the place. The longer we delay, the greater the chance the wounded will die."

"I know. It's too bad we didn't know they were coming this way so we could have headed them off."

"You can thank Agent Forbes for that," Summers said. "She totally mishandled this situation."

Gabe changed the subject, silently vowing to give her good marks when he wrote his own report. "So, are you planning to take adequate breaks tonight? I'll be glad to assign rangers to cover for you."

"Nobody covers for me," the agent said with rancor. "If I need your help, I'll ask for it."

Giving a casual salute and forcing a smile, Gabe bade him good-night and walked away. Strong will alone was not enough to sustain constant vigilance, no matter who was involved. Pride and hubris had brought down more than one determined man, himself included. As a green ranger he'd thought he was invincible. Now he knew otherwise. Part of doing his job well was being able to pace himself, to delegate responsibility to capable comrades when the need arose. And to back off for the sake of the mission. That was the hardest thing to learn. It was also called for in this case.

Thinking of Holly saddened him. She'd already done far more than was asked of her, yet her unorthodox methods were likely to sink her. Gabe sighed. With her sunny disposition and quick wit, she would have made a great public relations ranger. The way she related to children was amazing. All the campfire talks in the world couldn't compare to the way she connected to people, made them listen to her and take her teaching to heart.

Well, if the FBI didn't appreciate her natural talents, he certainly did. If he'd been an agent instead of a ranger, he'd have made sure their superiors were informed on a regular basis what a rare treasure she was.

His steps carried him past a group of sleeping rangers. And Holly. To his relief, she'd actually dozed off atop her sleeping bag. To his dismay, she looked so lovely, his heart hurt.

Pausing, he drank in the sight of her. This assignment was going to be one to remember, for sure. Would she recall him as fondly? Probably not. That didn't matter. There had been few instances in his life when circumstances— or a person—had imprinted his memory so well.

The camp was far from silent. Although nature had quieted down, the human element continued to stir. Beams from flashlights and camping lanterns shone among the sparse native trees and along the trails to and from the lodge. Moonlight came and went as clouds drifted across the sky, temporarily masking a celestial display unequaled in populated areas. Spirit Ranch was a special place. A sanctuary from the usual troubles of the world. Except right now. The overnight guests at the lodge were separated from his station's woes but they were surely being affected by the tense atmosphere in the bottom of the canyon.

Gabe sensed Holly stirring and looked down at her again. She was frowning. Her lips were moving in silent speech. Whatever dream was gripping her, it obviously wasn't a pleasant experience.

The longer he watched, the more agitated she became, tossing and turning as if fighting off invisible foes. He knew the nightmare would pass without his intervention and he'd intended to let it until she took a deep breath and opened her mouth wide, beginning to scream.

Gabe dropped to his knees. Clasped her wrists. "Easy, Christmas. It's okay. Just a bad dream."

That wasn't enough to comfort or fully awaken her. Struggling, she lashed out at him with her knees and feet.

He took the glancing blows and kept talking to her. "Holly! Wake up. It's okay. You're safe."

By this time most of the others nearby were awake and staring. "Bad dream," Gabe announced, knowing how odd it looked. "She's okay."

Her eyes wide, she seemed to finally focus on him. The struggling stopped and he released her. Tears glistened. Gabe was about to ask her to vouch for his innocence when she proved it without a doubt by throwing her arms around his neck and pulling herself to her knees in a clumsy hug.

Gabe was forced to return the embrace to keep his balance, not that he didn't want to provide all the comfort he could. Other people on the ground around them were lying back and relaxing. Someone gave a theatrical sigh. Someone else made exaggerated kissing sounds.

Gabe's brain told him to push her away and leave. His heart didn't agree. He did, however, loosen her grip on his neck and keep hold of her hands. "You had a bad dream."

"I...remember."

"Want to tell me about it?"

Judging by the way she was grasping his hands, the answer was yes. Then she glanced past his shoulder and gasped.

"There! Look!"

Gabe twisted to see. Nothing behind him was moving. He looked back to Holly and saw abject fear. "What? What do you think you saw?"

"Him. Them. The guys that were by the raft." She was choking back sobs, struggling to speak. "Right over there."

"There's nobody there but my people. You must have dreamed it."

Rapidly shaking her head, Holly stared into his eyes as if begging him to believe her when she said, "No! They were real."

"All right. You rest. I'll go check out that area."

Gabe stood and waited until she had eased back down. Then he nodded good-night and left her, pausing twice more to turn and make sure she had stayed where she was, safely surrounded by dozing rangers. There wasn't a safer place for her at present and although he did intend to keep his vow and check in the direction she'd indicated, he didn't expect to find interlopers.

They had tightened up the crime scene's perimeters and everyone inside the loop had been vetted. No loose thugs were lurking close by. The only real threats to Holly or anyone else were trapped inside the ranger station.

Hair at the back of Gabe's neck prickled. He rubbed it with his hand, assuming bothersome gnats had been drawn by his flashlight. What was it Holly had said? Trust your instincts? Fine. His were telling him that danger waited nearby. Logic, however, was also reminding him that a warm night brought out all sorts of tiny flying insects.

Stepping closer to a tree he clicked off his light. Listened. Waited. The bugs began to look elsewhere.

Gabe absorbed the surrounding atmosphere, assuming that would settle his mind. Instead, it brought a sense of dread that made his skin crawl. Either Holly was right about impending trouble, or he had been unduly influenced by her state of panic.

He waited while his eyes adjusted to the darker surroundings. A few unidentified shadows moved, seemed to shift. A slight breeze was blowing through the canyon. He could smell cooking. Fuel from camp stoves. Fires burning and smoking in grills placed above mandatory protective tarps along the river.

"What now, God?" Gabe whispered. "Which way?"

He heard a disturbance, looked back at the area where he'd left Holly. Something was causing a stir. He didn't have to actually see her to know the awful truth in his heart.

She was in trouble!

TWELVE

Holly tried to scream despite the large hand clamped over her mouth. She kicked hard, but she'd been sleeping barefoot, so no heavy hiking boots supported the effort.

Writhing and twisting was quickly tiring her so she purposely went limp, forcing her abductors to carry her and making her wish she weighed a lot more.

Voices were raising the alarm. Lights began to snap on all around them. Somebody else grasped her ankle in passing but failed to hang on.

And then she and her captors were in the clear. One was running, holding her head against his shoulder by covering her mouth and lifting her off the ground with an arm tight around her midsection. The other followed, ready to fend off rescuers. She could barely breathe.

Unfamiliar with the passing terrain, particularly after dark, Holly could only guess where she was being taken or who had grabbed her, but she had a feeling this was connected to the ongoing hostage situation. That did not bode well for her survival, particularly if this crook knew who she was, where she'd come from and why.

The shouting from behind them was getting louder. She tried to scream but it was muffled by the large hand over her mouth. When that didn't work, she bared her teeth enough to nip his palm. Cursing, the man let go long enough for her to let out one mighty "Help!"

They slid down a bank of red mud, landing on a sort of beach next to a natural cove off the main river course. Holly's spirits fell as the clouds parted and the moon lit the scene. Others were already assembled around an inflatable raft. One was balding and slightly portly. Another sported cargo shorts and a polo shirt but spoiled his disguise with black socks and dress shoes. The third, apparently a surviving cartel bigwig, too, was cringing behind the others. She guessed he was the accountant they'd dragged into their organization.

The river workers she'd originally reported as seeming out of place must be her captors. No wonder they were so strong. Whoever had decided the criminals could effectively escape by river, however, was delusional. If they somehow managed to negotiate the series of rapids without drowning or sinking, they'd still face officers of the law when they finally went ashore. They couldn't win.

The urge to announce that was strong. But her survival instinct was stronger. In order to have the slightest chance to get away, they'd need a hostage, and judging by the situation she found herself in, she was it. Therefore, they would want to keep her in good shape—at least for the present. And the longer she lived, the greater her chance of rescue.

Irony made her huff. She'd done exactly as Gabe had instructed and had ended up abducted. So much for ignoring instinct in favor of keeping strict rules.

Silent, breathless and trembling, Holly waited and listened. The more she learned about these men's plans, the better. She briefly studied each face in the waning moonlight. The two suspicious characters she'd spotted working on the raft were well muscled, stoic, recent additions. There were also the three dressed like tourists plus one more man she hadn't noticed at first. He looked and acted injured. Obviously her surviving drug cartel suspects had enlisted help to escape, and the injured man was their victim, a hostage like her, likely the ranger Gabe had told her about.

One of the two rivermen tied her wrists together in front of her and started dragging her toward the raft. The injured ranger was already there and she desperately hoped he would place her close enough to speak to him, so she used reverse psychology and began to struggle. "No. Not in the raft. I can't swim! Please, don't do this."

Laughing, he gave her a push and it was all Holly could do to keep from feeling smug. She flopped down in the slippery bottom of the inflatable, ending up very near to the youngish man holding his stomach despite also being bound. Because he was doubled over in pain and she was on the floor of the raft, she was able to speak to him covertly.

"I'm Holly Forbes, a friend of Gabe's," she whispered.

Although he didn't acknowledge her immediately, he did raise his head slightly. The anguish in his expression would have touched her even if he'd been a criminal.

"Anson Crawford," he breathed.

"Ranger?"

Anson nodded.

She touched his damp brow. He was burning up. "I'll try to get them to release you," Holly vowed. "You're in no condition to ride the river. You need medical care."

"Let them take me and save yourself," he managed,

teeth clenching as a wave of pain shot through him. "I'll be okay."

"Nonsense." Holly stood to get attention. "This man is in bad shape. You have me now. You don't need him."

One of the thugs guffawed. "Two's better than one. If he croaks, we'll still have you."

"If he dies, you'll stand trial for murder," she countered angrily. "And if you don't put him ashore, you'll get no cooperation out of me."

"Who says we need it?"

"Who says you don't?" To her relief the men formed a loose circle and began to argue among themselves. It was easy to tell that their opinions clashed. The more mature of them were all for getting rid of the injured man. The younger ones wanted to keep Anson, regardless of his condition.

Holly was certain they were about to decide in favor of her plan when several rangers burst out of the trees at a dead run.

Gabe McClellan was in the lead.

Holly saw the criminal closest to her take aim at the approaching rescuers. Bound, she nevertheless managed to throw herself at him, collide with his knees and spoil his aim.

To say he was upset was an understatement. Roaring, he turned the gun on her.

Holly curled up, raised her hands together in front of her face and waited for the lethal shot to explode through her.

Several others fired but no bullets came her way. When she looked up, she saw her adversary reeling. Bright red blood was pulsing from his shoulder. Remembering her medical training, she guessed someone had hit the subclavian artery. If so, he didn't have long to live.

The man dropped to his knees beside her, then tried to crawl aboard the raft with one arm as his companions hurriedly pushed it into the water.

Holly was hauled to her feet by the criminal she had knocked into, and literally thrown back in over the inflated side, hitting herself on one of the two solid bench seats with such force it knocked the breath out of her. All she could think about was whether Gabe was okay. She had to know he hadn't been shot.

It took three tries for her to get her balance enough to look. Her heart leaped with joy. Not only was he unhurt, he was waving his arms to direct his men and they were closing in.

She heard him holler, "Hold your fire!"

Assuming he now had control of the situation, she tried to catch her breath and thanked God for deliverance. That peace was short-lived. Someone grabbed a handful of her hair and hauled her to her feet, using her as a human shield.

Eyes wide, she stared at Gabe. His expression was stern but beneath the surface, she saw angst. And perhaps personal concern.

When someone finally spoke, it was Gabe. "Let her go. I'll go with you in her place."

Holly shouted, "No!"

The thug holding her laughed. "Tell you what I will do. I'll trade this useless ranger for an able-bodied one. The girl stays with us."

"Done," Gabe said. Without hesitation he ordered his men to stand down, placed his gun on the ground at his feet and raised his hands. "Set him onshore and I'll join you."

Holly's head was pounding. What could she do? She'd begged for medical aid for the wounded man and he was about to receive it. But she didn't want it to be at Gabe's expense. *Please, Lord, not at Gabe's expense.*

The man who was holding her up gestured with a pistol and two of his companions off-loaded the injured ranger, placing him beside the fallen thug.

Tears filled Holly's eyes, then slid down her cheeks. She was frightened. And ashamed, because part of her was actually glad that Gabe would be in the raft with her. That was so selfish she was filled with self-loathing, yet nothing changed the fact that she was not going to be alone. Someone she trusted, admired and cared for was going to be with her. Solo, she might have been tempted to give up. With Gabe beside her, she'd have both moral and tactical support.

Together…together, they would survive. Somehow. God willing.

One of the four remaining men began passing out bright orange life jackets as the raft drifted from the shore in the shallows and began to bob. Gabe accepted one and said, "I'll have to untie the woman to put this on her."

The largest of his captors laughed. "Sorry. We only brought enough for the rest of us. Since you shot my friend, you get to wear his."

Gabe considered refusing the vest, then reconsidered. If he washed overboard and drowned, there would be nobody left to help Holly. He had no choice.

Glancing at her, he felt his heart swell with pride, then crack from seeing her scratches and bruises—and tears. The fondness he had acknowledged before was growing by the second as he considered the possibility of losing her forever. Regardless of whether or not they ever grew as close as he now hoped they would, she must be rescued. There was no other acceptable outcome.

"All right," Gabe said. Gazing deeply into Holly's glistening eyes while hoping and praying she would understand, he donned and fastened the life vest.

With a barely perceptible nod she proved she did.

The thug gestured with a pistol. "Take the oars."

"Who, me?"

His armed adversary was not amused. "Yes, you. I can't row and steer and keep you covered at the same time. You shot my buddy. You're taking his place."

Gabe took the seat between the oarlocks and began to propel the small raft into the current. Holly had told him the four she was after were city types. One had died in the flash flood. That left three novices, so even if the raft wrecked by accident he couldn't be certain they'd survive.

He shouted at the closest guy. "You wanna live through this, you'll pass out those helmets and wear one, too. If we hit the rocks, we can die of concussions. Vests keep you afloat but they don't do anything to protect your head."

The slightly built, middle-aged man was trembling so badly he could hardly pick up a helmet for himself, let alone pass around others.

"Give one to the woman," Gabe said. Now that the current was moving them, he shipped the oars and sat back. "Assuming you all want me to keep steering."

The armed man gave a gruff okay. "Just do it."

The raft was already slewing sideways, and by the time Holly had managed to fasten the snap with her wrists tied it was almost crossways of the flow.

The gun pointed at Gabe. "All right. Get busy. I plan to survive this trip, even if you don't." He scowled. "I don't know what these other guys did but I just met them yesterday. They called my cousin and hired us for a pickup at Spirit Station, okay?"

Gabe shot a quick glance toward Holly. Did she want him to explain or keep quiet? Logic could have argued both ways. Then, she nodded solemnly and began to speak.

"They're wanted for attempted murder in Las Vegas," she said, raising her voice to be heard over the approaching noise of tumbling, falling water. "If you didn't know they were fugitives, why did you come armed? And why do you think they wanted to leave in the dark?"

Gabe didn't expect a response. The presence of a wounded National Park Ranger would have been enough evidence to tip off even the most clueless crooks. This rafter was not an innocent bystander. He and his injured friend were complicit in a crime and knew it. Like it or not, he and Holly Forbes were prisoners of at least one hardened criminal and three others wanted for murder, racing toward dangerous rapids.

If he had been the only captive, he could have let the craft flounder in the turbulent water and taken his chances, but because of Holly that was not an option. This journey was a level five out of five, indicating the most difficult and challenging of white-water trips. And they were just getting started.

"Untie the woman in case I need her to shift her weight to balance us," Gabe shouted.

"You take me for a fool?" the armed man asked. "I can just shoot her and pitch her overboard if she's a problem." He was perched in the bow, facing backward, while the cartel survivors grouped in the rear and Holly occupied a place just to Gabe's right and the gunman's left.

She was in a cramped position, pushing her feet against the floor and her back against the inflated side to try to maintain her position. The wetter the side got, the slipperier it became. Her helmet hid her face until she lifted her head and caught Gabe's eye for a split second.

That was the instant he comprehended. He shook his head, hoping it was enough for Holly and praying the gunman didn't notice.

She mouthed the word *yes*.

"No," he insisted.

Again, she cast her gaze over the side, pushing and inching up, taking advantage of the tilt when he guided the raft over smaller rocks to avoid smashing into boulders. Gabe imagined what she must be thinking and disagreed so strongly it tied his gut in knots.

Watching the rapids and handling the raft to the best of his ability took so much concentration, he missed seeing her gain the top of the wide, rubber outside rim.

And then there she was, poised to put her daring idea into play. He saw her keeping an eye on the gunman. And him. And the river ahead. She was going to do it. She was going to jump.

THIRTEEN

Holly balanced precariously on the slick rim and waited for the right moment. After the recent rains the river was muddy. That would help hide her but it would also keep Gabe from finding her if she threw herself into the bone-chilling waters.

She had to turn sideways to grasp the safety ropes strung along the raft's sides since her hands were still tied together. Every time she'd thought she was unobserved, she'd worked to untie the knots but they'd refused to budge.

Her gaze kept darting to Gabe, and the few times when their eyes met she willed him to understand. Determination was radiating from him. Arm muscles rippled beneath the sleeves of his wet shirt. He demonstrated perfect balance in spite of the pitching and rolling of the flexible raft, while it took all her remaining strength to hang on and keep from being flung out before she was ready. She jogged daily and kept in good physical shape but being bound was putting added demand on her stamina, and she wondered how long it would be before she was forced to let go and ended up floundering in the river.

The raft rose to meet a surge, then dropped into a

trough. Waves topped the bow and washed over everyone, including the gunman. A quick glance at the water directly ahead gave her hope. *Now!*

The last thing Holly saw before she shut her eyes tightly and leaned backward was the shock on Gabe's face, and she wished she'd had a chance to bid him a fond goodbye. This was the right thing to do. She was positive.

Cold slammed into her as if slivers of ice were piercing her skin. An instant migraine made her dizzy and nauseous. Frigid water swirled around her, sucking her down and leaving her unsure which way was up. Which way held the air she so desperately needed.

She opened her eyes to nothing but murky brown water. With her hands raised in front of her face to protect against crashing headfirst into a giant boulder, she kicked away. There was a chance that the raft was still close by and what the gunman might do was unknown. If he fired blindly into the torrent, she might accidentally be hit.

A sudden surge of current slammed her sideways into a pile of rocks, knocking the last of her breath out of her. Desperate, she grabbed at anything her fingers touched and realized her momentum had been slowed by the collision.

Bringing her knees under her, she tried to stand, to reach the surface. It wasn't quite enough but it did give her direction. That was all she needed.

She kicked as hard as she could. For long seconds she doubted it was helping. Then she broke the surface and began coughing. Somebody yelled. The helmet had protected her enough to avoid a concussion but it also dampened sound. Which way?

Bobbing like a cork, she realized it didn't really matter much unless she survived. Her body was already so cold her muscles were starting to quit working properly and she wore no life vest to keep her afloat. Soon, hypothermia would cast her adrift like one of the pieces of dead wood hikers gathered to burn in their campfires.

Holly's thoughts centered on Gabe and she whispered as if he could hear, "I'm sorry we never had the chance to fall in love."

Anticipating Holly's reckless move and dreading the probable consequences, Gabe had been ready. He'd seen her lean as the onrushing wave covered the bow and had made her move. She'd disappeared into the rushing, roiling brown water as if she'd never existed.

Gasping as deep a breath as he could on short notice, he'd released the oars, shoved them aside and followed her into the frigid, unforgiving waters of the Colorado.

When he had abandoned the raft he'd assumed it would begin to swerve and bounce, disorienting its remaining occupants. If the armed man moved to the oars quickly enough, he could probably regain control in time to prevent an accident. If, however, he concentrated on shooting at the people in the water instead, his whole party would likely be doomed.

Gabe's vest kept pushing him toward the surface as he sought some sign of Holly. *Please, God, help me!* began as a silent plea, then out loud as he broke the surface. "Please, God!"

Moonlight glistened off the waves except where patches of white water distorted the scene. He blinked to clear his vision. Off to the left and bouncing downriver at top speed, the gray raft was already way ahead of him.

"Holly!" Floating and kicking himself in a full circle,

he looked and looked. His spirits plummeted. "Holly! Where are you?"

A faint reply seemed to drift on the wind but the noise of the passing water was muting it. He called again. "Holleee!"

Then he heard it. His name. And it had never sounded sweeter. "Holly!" Gabe yelled. "Where are you?"

It was impossible to comprehend her words but the direction was becoming clearer. Half bouncing in the waves, half swimming, he worked his way toward her. Spotted her yellow helmet next to a drift of rocks. Then lost sight of it.

Hard strokes and kicks carried him closer. There were the rocks but where was Holly? He hauled himself up onto the pile to check downstream. No sign of the helmet.

Without a life vest she could have been pulled under! And while he still wore his, his chances of diving down to her were hampered. There was no choice but one. He unbuckled the vest, threw it onto the upper rocks in the hopes it would stay there, then filled his lungs with air and dived in.

There was no strength and little hope left in Holly's heart and mind. The moment she'd realized that Gabe had escaped it was as if she'd received permission to relax. To finally join her sister in heaven. That was where she belonged. With Ivy. Telling her how sorry she was for being such a selfish brat and abandoning her to a horrible fate.

Thoughts spun in and out of Holly's head at dizzying speed. She saw herself young, then older, then as a child again. And during all that time she knew she was loved. That was true even in the period after losing Ivy, she realized, feeling grateful and at peace.

Lungs bursting, she knew surrender was imminent. But Gabe. What about Gabe? Would he blame himself the way she had taken the blame for losing her sister?

Picturing him grieving gave her a momentary burst of strength, of renewed will. Raising her bound hands overhead, she started to kick and felt the water lifting, spinning, bearing her along sideways as if intent on returning her to the open channel.

Something grabbed her wrist, pulled her all the way up. She gasped for air. Coughing, gagging and spitting water.

Strong arms encircled her waist and turned her. It was Gabe! Of course it was. How he had found her when he had was a mystery of gigantic proportions. He had accomplished the impossible, and for that she would be thankful for the rest of her life—to him and to their heavenly Father.

Stroking sideways toward the rock ridge that had slowed her drift, Gabe delivered Holly and himself to the rocks where she hoped they could recoup. If they didn't freeze to death. She couldn't stop shivering no matter how hard she tried.

Gabe untied her wrists, reached for the discarded vest and tried to put it on her. "No. N-no. You."

"I don't need it. You have hypothermia."

"We…" Holly's teeth literally chattered. She couldn't believe anybody could ever get this cold. Unable to fully explain, she wrapped her arms around his waist and laid her icy cheek on his chest. If that didn't tell him what she wanted him to do, nothing would.

Thankfully, Gabe got the idea. He donned the soggy vest, pulled her close and wrapped it around her as best he could.

Holly hung on, thrilled to be alive but wondering how much longer either of them would survive being so wet and cold. By this time she could tell that Gabe was trembling, too. If he lost his grip or if the dam released more water or if it took the rangers too long to rescue them, they might be nearing the end of both their lives.

There were too many variables. She needed to speak her mind, not wait for a later time that might never come.

A shaky breath, then another, was barely enough, yet she tried. "Gabe?"

"It's all right, honey. I've got you."

"I know, but…"

"Hush. Save your strength."

"N-no."

His hold tightened and she reciprocated by snuggling closer. Perhaps it was better if she didn't look at his face while she confessed her feelings. The way she felt at the moment, his rejection might be enough to steal the last dregs of hope.

Holding tight and speaking against his wet shirt, she managed to say "I love you" without coughing.

"I think you're pretty special, too, Christmas."

"I…love…"

"I got that. A simple thanks will suffice."

She moved one arm out from beneath the vest just long enough to slap him on the chest.

Gabe's embrace tightened around her and he began to rub her back through the side of the vest. "Warm up, come to your senses and tell me all about it later if you still want to, okay?"

A slightly different motion added to his shivers and it took Holly a moment to realize he was either laughing or crying. She wasn't sure which, and she figured either could be good so she didn't try to look.

They were still huddled atop the rocks when the ranger rescue raft reached them twenty minutes later. Holly resisted being hauled aboard first but finally gave in. Gabe was going to be all right, too. They'd survived the worst night of their lives and imminent death.

Plus, she had told him she loved him. Not only was it time to wrap up her case and get ready to leave the park, she was going to be doing it red-faced with embarrassment. Particularly if he failed to express any romantic interest in her before she went back to Las Vegas.

Huddled beneath blankets and drinking hot chocolate from a thermos, Gabe asked the other rangers for a briefing.

"We fished out two of the three cartel guys and the owner of the gray raft," Broadstreet said. "Hough is waiting for us at the Whitmore helipad. You're not nearly as far downriver as we thought you'd be."

Gabe glanced over at the quivering pile of blankets that was Holly Forbes. "We decided to get off early when the guy with the gun threatened to shoot us."

"I thought he wanted a hostage."

"Yeah, well…" Gabe tilted his head toward the exasperating woman who had nearly gotten them both killed. "My FBI partner fell out so I jumped in after her. The others were all wearing life jackets but they didn't give one to her."

"It's a wonder you found her with the river so muddy," the other ranger said.

Gabe sobered and sighed. "Yeah, I know."

Thinking back, he didn't know how he'd managed to locate her, let alone find a place where they could climb out and wait for help. The only thing that would have surprised him more was to have been tossed up onshore together, dry. Whatever he had prayed while he'd searched the frigid water must have been the best plea he'd ever made. Or the simplest. When he'd seen her disappear under the water, his heart had called out with such desperate fervor he suspected that that alone had been sufficient.

Sitting on the rocks and holding Holly close, he'd had plenty of time to think about everything she'd told him. The FBI was her life. So be it. As long as he could continue to uphold the law, he supposed he could do it anywhere, even in a city, as long as he got the chance to become a part of her world.

They'd be transported to a hospital for observation and treatment as a matter of procedure. While he was there he'd have time and opportunity to look into changing jobs. It was risky but doable. Holly was worth any sacrifice. He huffed. "Yeah, even almost drowning."

EPILOGUE

Leaving Grand Canyon National Park in a medical chopper was not the way Holly had intended to depart. Agent Andrew Summers had finished up the case while she was being treated in Las Vegas, and her bosses had informed her she was being put on temporary leave. Good or bad, it was nonnegotiable.

Her fondest hope was that the final reports had not painted too vivid a picture of her actions on this particular assignment because the more she thought about Gabe and working outdoors in such natural beauty, the more she felt dissatisfied with her FBI position.

Having her heart finally at peace regarding Ivy helped, of course, but the driving force behind her choice to resign was the hope she would qualify for a law enforcement position with the National Park Service. Joining the Forest Service wouldn't do. It wasn't the same thing. It had to be national parks. And somehow, she'd have to figure out how to arrange placement near the Grand Canyon. Yes, she knew she might as well try to become an astronaut or earn the pole position at the Indy 500, but she'd never know if she didn't at least try.

The paperwork was in and Holly was waiting impatiently for word. Any word. Just something. When she got tired of pacing the floor, waiting for a call and watching her email, she packed clothes and a few camping things in her car and headed west.

"Don't scold him for not calling you," she lectured herself as she drove. "It's not like you called him, either."

Because I want to see him in person, she thought. That was going to tell her more than any phone call, even if they used a video connection.

The closer Holly got to the park entrance, the more nervous she became. Nevertheless, she drove straight to ranger headquarters on the south rim, parked and went inside.

Tourists crowded the large room filled with information and pictures of the canyon, including portraits of all the current rangers. She located Gabe's picture and stood in front of it, while her heart raced. There were no more prayers that needed saying, no more wishes to make and no more time to waste. Either he was interested or he wasn't. Simple as that. She'd come to face him and that was exactly what she was going to do.

A familiar reflection appeared in the glass covering the portrait. Holly whirled and almost threw herself into Gabe's arms. Her hands clamped on the strap of her shoulder bag and she grinned up at him. "Hi."

"Hi, yourself. What brings you back?"

"I had to come," she confessed. "I left something here."

He arched an eyebrow. "Oh? What?"

She tried to wet her dry lips and failed. This was it. Sink or swim, so to speak. Finally she gathered the courage to say, "My heart."

"Let's go into my office," he said, cupping her elbow. "I have a surprise for you."

"A good one?"

He guided her through the door and closed it behind them, then indicated a chair in front of the desk while he circled it to sit in his own place. "I think it's good. We'll see what you think in a minute."

"Nice office," Holly remarked, nervous about what he might be planning to reveal. If he announced something like an engagement to some other woman she knew she'd shatter.

"I've liked it here. But I think I'll adjust well wherever I go."

She sat forward, frowning. "What do you mean, *wherever you go*? If you're thinking of transferring, it will ruin everything."

"Ruin what? It's my decision, Holly. The only one that made sense after I met you." He rose, then approached and perched a hip on the corner of his desk so he could reach for her hand.

"But…but you can't. I've already resigned and…"

Gabe's jaw dropped. "You *what*?"

"Resigned. Left the FBI. I'm waiting to hear that I've been approved for training as a National Park Ranger." Her voice trembled. "I wanted to be near you, just in case we… I mean, I… Oh, I don't know what I mean."

Instead of continued shock, she saw amusement flooding his countenance and he began to laugh. Soon, he was nearly roaring and tears of joy were running down his cheeks.

She bristled. "What's so funny? I was good at the job when I volunteered and I have professional law enforcement training now. Why shouldn't I become a ranger?"

Gabe cleared his throat and coughed. "Because I've applied to join the FBI."

"You what? Why? You love this job."

He took her hand and held it gently. "There is something I love more."

"How could you? I mean, we hardly know each other."

Gabe nodded and pulled her to her feet. "I get that. I really do. But I figured if we both worked for the FBI, we could take it slower and get better acquainted."

"That's why I wanted to be a ranger!"

"Shall we toss a coin?"

Holly was shaking her head. "Nope. I went into the FBI for the wrong reasons. What I recently realized is that I've always wanted to be a ranger."

"I can't be your boss and still date you," Gabe warned.

"Then recommend I be put into public relations or make me a museum guide. I don't care. I can hardly wait to leave the city and come back to nature." She blushed and lowered her voice. "To come back to you."

Lips trembling, heart racing, she lifted her face and waited for him to make the next move.

Gabe smiled. And then he kissed her.

And she kissed him back.

* * * * *

Dear Reader,

I've visited most of our national parks except for those in Hawaii, and each has its own unique beauty. The Grand Canyon is famous, yes, but there is so much more to it than what you see standing on the edge looking down.

Likewise, there is much more to the job of a National Park Ranger than what you might see on the surface. Researching for this novella really taught me a lot and opened my eyes to the trials as well as heroic actions of men and women who are, for the most part, underestimated by the general public. I will never look at someone wearing that uniform or the Smoky Bear hat in the same way again.

As Holly learned, divine forgiveness is waiting for you regardless of what mistakes you might have made in the past. Turn your regrets over to the Lord and He will help you forgive yourself, too.

Blessings,
Valerie Hansen

Email: val@valeriehansen.com

MISSING IN THE WILDERNESS

Jodie Bailey

To Chip,
You believed in a no-name Carolina girl
with a NASCAR novel.
You've been a great agent, friend and mentor.
Thank you.

I will lift up mine eyes unto the hills, from whence cometh my help. My help cometh from the Lord, which made heaven and earth. He will not suffer thy foot to be moved: he that keepeth thee will not slumber.
—Psalm 121:1-3

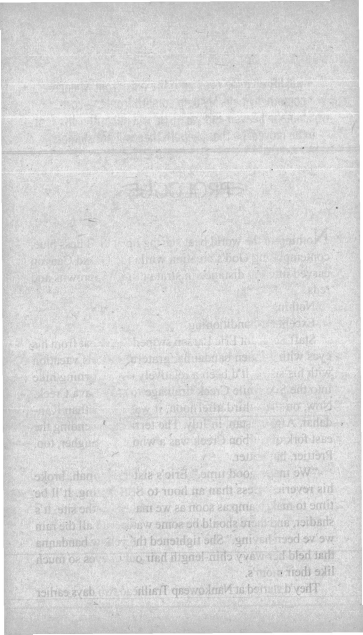

PROLOGUE

Nothing in the world beat staring up at cloudless blue, contemplating God's creation while the Grand Canyon carved into the distance in strata of grays, browns and reds.

Nothing.

Except air-conditioning.

Staff Sergeant Eric Larson swiped the sweat from his eyes with a green bandanna, grateful for this vacation with his sister. It'd been a relatively easy morning hike into the Sixtymile Creek drainage toward Lava Creek. Now, on their third afternoon, it was hotter than Kandahar, Afghanistan, in July. The terrain descending the east fork of Carbon Creek was a whole lot rougher, too. Prettier, but hotter.

"We made good time." Eric's sister, Hannah, broke his reverie. "Less than an hour to Still Spring. It'll be time to make camp as soon as we make it to the site. It's shadier, and there should be some water with all the rain we've been having." She tightened the yellow bandanna that held her wavy chin-length hair out of eyes so much like their mom's.

They'd started at Nankoweap Trailhead two days earlier

and had descended several thousand feet, going off trail through the backcountry most of the way.

Descended was a tricky word. It was more like down, up, over and around so many outcroppings and rock-strewn animal trails he'd lost count. Some of day one's ledges had challenged even his battle-hardened bravado.

But the view? With the canyon spreading into the distant horizon? Worth every aching muscle.

Hannah tightened her pack for the last descent to the spot they'd laid out months ago for this night in the back-country. "You still glad we're doing this?"

"Totally." He fell into step behind her. They'd spent his entire yearlong deployment planning this trip, emailing details and websites back and forth, and shipping travel books to one another. They'd been hiking the Grand Canyon together once a year for a decade ever since their parents died in a boating accident on the Colorado River. They'd started with the more well-known and well-traveled Bright Angel and South Kaibab Trails. This trek from Nankoweap Trailhead on the North Rim to Bright Angel at the South Rim was a solitary nine-day haul. They'd probably not see another person until day seven or eight. It was the most ambitious trip they'd planned yet.

It was also some of the most incredible country Eric had ever seen. After a year overseas, his thirty days of postdeployment leave were well spent with his sister in and around the canyon. It was home. Their parents had been National Park Service rangers who had taught their children to love and respect God's creation.

Lately, the desire to follow in their footsteps was strong. If he made the leap and joined the Park Service, maybe he could get stationed somewhere closer to Hannah.

Though the Grand Canyon itself was out of the question due to a certain ex-wife of his who was stationed here. He'd settle for their annual pilgrimage.

"What's your plan to top this next year?" It was possible to get more remote, but it would be tough.

Hannah glanced over her shoulder at him, then turned her attention to the front. "This is year ten for us, big brother." Yeah, big brother by seven whole minutes. "Ten is a nice, even kind of number. Sort of like a completion. What do you say next we tackle another park? A different adventure?"

What? Eric's foot slid on loose rock and he righted himself, focusing on what passed for a trail. This annual trip was a way to keep alive the adventurous spirit their parents had instilled in them. Hannah's wanting to change the location was huge.

While the hikes were a kind of cleansing for him, they seemed to drag Hannah into the past. She generally shed a tear or two when they reached the Colorado River. Eric was less expressive, though he felt the emotion.

A skittering sound behind him broke his thoughts. Small rocks and pebbles tumbled past his feet, knocked loose from above. Eric stopped and turned, scanning the area they'd traversed. Nothing but scrub brush and a few trees that barely deserved the name.

Maybe an animal? He touched the Glock at his side. It was rare for anybody in the backcountry to be attacked by a large animal. Rock squirrel bites seemed to be the biggest issue. Still, he felt a whole lot better with protection, especially since keeping Hannah safe was now his responsibility alone.

For ten minutes, they hiked silently to Lava Creek,

searching for a spot with enough water to replenish their supply and enough flat space to bunk for the night.

The hairs on the back of Eric's neck stood up the whole time, and not in a rock-squirrel kind of way. He'd hiked too many mountains in Afghanistan in full battle rattle while wrestling with this feeling.

Of being watched. Of human eyes on him. The feeling something very bad was about to happen.

He'd been right every time.

It was impossible. They were literally in the middle of nowhere, and it was highly unlikely there was another soul within dozens of miles. The crime rate at the canyon wasn't high and was concentrated around the populated areas.

No one was stalking them in this deserted land. He'd been deployed too long, hadn't been home in the States long enough for the paranoia to wane. It was possible being in the canyon triggered reminders of the Afghan mountains.

Even though they looked nothing alike.

They'd reached a flat spot on the rocks near Still Spring before he relaxed. Recent rains had the creeks running higher than usual, though that wasn't saying much. Refilling water and washing up would be a little easier than in times past, when they'd had to settle for trickles in drier seasons.

Hannah knelt and splashed her face, soaking her yellow bandanna and scrubbing it across her neck. "You've been quiet. It's okay if you want to keep hiking the canyon for a few more years. I feel like…" She rocked back on her heels and stared at the multicolored rocks and boulders along the creek bed. "I feel like it's time."

Crouching beside her, Eric dragged his bandanna

through the water and wrung it out over his head. Sweet relief. He hadn't been this filthy in weeks. "It's a good idea. And it's time. What are you thinking?"

"Yellowstone."

"Mom's first assignment as a ranger." He should have known. It had been in Yellowstone that vacationing ranger Rob Larson had met Kim Register and convinced her they could make a life at his duty station in the Grand Canyon. She'd applied for a transfer before his vacation was over and the rest...

The rest was Eric and Hannah's history.

Her cheeks pinked, and she pushed her hands against her knees, standing and turning toward a bend in the creek. "Yes, but it's Yellowstone. It's been a long time since I've been out of the desert Southwest. Who knows? Maybe someday we'll hike some Icelandic glaciers or something."

"You'd better marry someone as adventurous as you are."

"Far as I'm concerned, if a man can keep up with me, he can marry me." Hannah tossed a teasing grin over her shoulder and aimed a finger at a bend in the creek. "I'm going to explore, see if I can find the old coffee grinder that's been around so long a cottonwood grew around it."

Hannah's life goal was to join one of the rare archaeological digs in the canyon. Her doctoral studies had concentrated on the area. One more reason her desire to branch out was a shocker.

She started toward the creek. "If I need an adventurous man, you're going to need an equally adventurous woman."

He yelled at her retreating back as she disappeared around the bend. "Never getting married." *Again.*

"We'll see!" Her call echoed, the tone lighthearted.

The words were an indictment he'd never discussed with anyone, not even his sister.

Because he had been married...once. To a young National Park Service ranger who'd helped search for his parents. The grief of his loss coupled with her loneliness at an assignment to this new and wild place had fueled a whirlwind of dating. It had culminated in a marriage of less than a year. His life stationed at Fort Bliss near El Paso and hers in the canyon had worked against them. His career was the army, and hers was the Park Service. Neither would budge.

While Hannah had met Morgan, he'd never told his sister about their marriage. Initially, he knew she'd question his rush to the altar. Foolishness and pride had kept him quiet ever since.

He thought of Morgan daily, but more intensely on these hikes. Morgan Dunham was still a park ranger here, and he spent little time in public areas to avoid seeing her.

Eric lay on the flat rock, closed his eyes and let the still, hot air bake away the aches in his joints.

If things had been different, he could have loved Morgan forever. That was probably why he took serious pains to avoid her. She was the kind of woman who would make a soldier question his life choices.

After this last deployment, some of those decisions looked a lot like taking a job in a remote park where nobody shot at him or tried to blow him up. At thirty-one, the thought of another deployment sapped his mental and physical energy.

But right now, under the heat of the sun after a long day of hiking, peace bred a warm rest he couldn't fight.

A shift in the light sat him straight up, heart pounding. The sun had dipped, deepening the shadows around him. How long had he been asleep?

He glanced at his watch. Over an hour. Why had Hannah let him sleep? They had to make camp before dark and—

Hannah.

Eric sprang to his feet so fast, head swimming with heat. His sister hadn't returned. Her pack still sat where she'd left it.

His heart drove faster as he jogged toward the creek bend, calling her name over and over, echoes overlapping his shouts.

Past the bend, in the mud at the edge of the creek, there were boot prints that disappeared at the water's edge.

And a yellow bandanna lying at the edge of the shallow water.

ONE

"I'm sorry, Mr. Lanning. I can't comment on active investigations or searches, but I can put you through to Public Relations." Ranger Morgan Dunham glanced out of the small office into the lobby of the Backcountry Information Center. In the sunlit room, rangers answered questions or helped backpackers obtain permits for trips deep into the Grand Canyon.

If only she'd stepped in to help with the backlog instead of answering the phone. Brandon Lanning was a self-styled outdoor guru and blogger who had latched onto the disappearance of a female hiker two weeks earlier. He called multiple times a day, convinced there was a vast conspiracy "the people" needed to know about.

"All I want is an update on Hannah Larson. This is a high-profile missing-persons case."

Hannah had disappeared in the canyon two weeks earlier. While the circumstances were somewhat strange, it was far from "high profile." The mission had shifted from rescue to recovery, and resources had been assigned to other rescues and a troubling series of attacks on park rangers. Two rangers had been beaten at remote stations. Another had nearly been shoved off a ledge following a nature talk. Coupled with Hannah's disappearance, the park was on edge.

No way was she passing that on to Blogger Brandon.

She didn't want to talk about it with anyone. Hannah's disappearance was too personal. "I'm transferring you to Public Relations. Have a nice day." Morgan punched buttons, then settled the phone into its cradle.

Tomorrow, Morgan was headed out on a private search, using vacation time to hike an area outside the search grid.

Tapping a pen on the desk, she stared into the lobby. Hannah Larson. The name brought images of another time, another search... The search for the girl's parents had ended with the recovery of two bodies, miles apart, wrecked by the Colorado River's rapids.

Brought images of Hannah's brother, Eric, Morgan's ex-husband. The marriage had been short-lived, but the emotions ran high.

She'd met his sister only a handful of times, the first on the day Rangers Kim and Rob Larson were buried, the loss deep for the family and for the Park Service. Hannah had been at college when Eric proposed on the edge of the canyon less than a week later. Morgan should have recognized it for the fit of grief it was, should have realized she was reacting to her own loneliness as a newly minted ranger running from her past.

When Hannah disappeared, Morgan had been on a ten-day backcountry patrol miles away from the search area, unable to help. Now she'd had her mandatory four days of postpatrol rest and had taken leave starting tomorrow. She intended to spend the next two weeks on a private patrol.

While her marriage to Eric had flamed out quickly in a battle of distance and competing life goals, he deserved closure if the massive canyon had stolen his last living family member. And Morgan would do everything she could to help him find it…as long as she didn't have to actually lay eyes on him.

Half of her longed to find him and offer some comfort, but seeing him again might cause her to chuck her career and follow him wherever the army ordered. Not a day had passed in the last eight years when she hadn't lost herself at some point in the what-ifs of their failed attempt at a life together.

Morgan turned to the computer and moved the mouse, wiping away an image of a sunset over the canyon, and studied the gridded map laid out during the search. She zoomed in on the area around Still Spring, where Hannah had vanished, then sketched out a route along the Unkar Delta, one few of the searchers had chosen.

So much made no sense. Even with the recent rains, Lava Creek wasn't deep enough to sweep away a grown woman. Getting lost would have been hard unless Hannah was trying to disappear.

A couple of searchers had floated the idea Eric had killed his sister, but that didn't wash. There was no evidence, and Eric…

He'd never hurt Hannah.

But too many years had passed… Did Morgan know him anymore?

Had they really known each other to start with? Not only had they hidden their marriage from his sister, but she'd never shared her deepest fears with him, never shared the reason she'd left the police force to become a backcountry ranger. He'd have looked at her differently, would have shunned her like…

Not that it mattered. The walls between them had been higher than either of them had acknowledged.

And now, with his sister missing, she couldn't do anything for him except search.

She propped her chin on her balled fist, closed her eyes and prayed for Hannah's safety. Only God could provide after this amount of time. She asked God to guide and encourage searchers disheartened after a long trek with no resolution.

She prayed for Eric. *Lord, comfort him. Don't let him become bitter—*

"Morgan."

The sound of her name hit her ears like a rock slide. Her eyes tightened. It had to be imaginary, because that voice... It sounded like *his*.

"Morgan, open your eyes." The words cracked with exhaustion and uncertainty.

She counted to three. If no one was there, she was hallucinating, which meant a host of bad things. But if he was in front of her, life was about to get worse than a wild imagination.

Morgan looked up and rocketed to her feet, the sensation that her heart had lodged in her throat nearly choking her. "Eric." His name shattered into a whisper.

Eric Larson stood on the other side of the desk, still tall, even more muscular and with a face more chiseled and matured by time and experience. His brown hair was short and streaked by the sun. And his eyes... Those same brown eyes that had gazed at her with love and longing were now dark with grief and determination.

The woozy sensation of looking into the eyes of a stranger who had once been her husband almost rocked her off her feet. She gripped the edge of the desk and fought for some sort of professional control.

He said nothing, merely stared as though their reunion shook him, as well.

Morgan cleared her throat and found her voice first. "I'm sorry about Hannah." Aiming a finger at a chair on the other side of the desk, she sat and waited for him to do the same.

He glanced over his shoulder at the door, then studied her before he sat, tension cording his muscles. He watched her as though he expected something Morgan didn't know how to give him.

Still, he said nothing.

Morgan turned the computer screen toward him, desperate to break the tense silence. "I'm taking leave for two weeks and heading out tomorrow, checking out this area here." She stabbed a finger at the location she'd marked. "It's outside the search grid, but it won't hurt to—"

"They think I'm pushing myself too hard and they won't give me another permit to hike unless I have someone with me. I'm going with you."

The steel in his voice ran a chill along her arms. Hiking the backcountry with the man who'd very briefly been her entire world? The man who still haunted both her dreams and her waking thoughts?

No. Any other ranger in the park could take him. Several of them owed her favors. She was going out on her own without any dangerous proximity to Eric Larson.

Morgan dug her teeth into her lower lip. A direct denial would ramp up his stubborn streak. She needed a minute. "I thought you left this morning."

"And I thought you'd help me. Maybe I was wrong."

He leaped out of the chair and paced to the door, staring out into the lobby, his shoulders a tight line. "I'm sorry. This whole mess has me…" Eric returned and sank into the chair again, as though despair and defeat had liquefied his bones. His gaze rested on the floor between his feet. "I don't have anywhere else to go."

He'd worn the same lost-little-boy expression ten years ago, wrestling with the loss of his parents.

It had melted Morgan's heart.

She was eight years older and a broken marriage wiser now, but this man still squeezed her emotions. If Morgan still had the right, she'd round the desk, crouch in front of him and pull his head to her shoulder, let him share her strength.

But they'd signed away the right when they inked divorce papers. Although it was way beyond her better judgment, the best she could offer him was her time.

"I'm heading out from Nankoweap Trailhead at five thirty in the morning. Another ranger is dropping me off early so I can hike before the day gets too hot. Meet me there." There was no need to give him further instructions. She'd followed his journeys with Hannah every year, tracing their paper trail through the system. Eric knew what to pack and how to dress. He was also a meticulous planner and didn't need her babysitting him.

"Thank you." He lifted his gaze to meet hers briefly, then dropped it again. "I wouldn't be here if I had another option. I'd… I'd let you keep on living your life without my interference."

"I know." Morgan puffed out the breath she didn't realize she'd been holding. "I'll take care of having your permit updated and bring you a new one with me at the trailhead tomorrow. When was the last time you slept?"

Eric shook his head, his posture saying he might fall asleep in the chair if he didn't move soon. It was probably the first time he'd sat, the first time he'd allowed himself to remove some of the burden.

Rounding the desk, Morgan laid a hand on his shoulder, the first time she'd touched him in too many years. It was a memory and a touch she didn't allow to linger. "Come on. I'll walk you to your car. You're no good to Hannah if you land yourself in the hospital."

He stood and let her usher him into the lobby. At the exterior door, Morgan called over her shoulder to Ranger Mark Davis, "Be back in a minute."

He waved her away with a quick glance and an approving nod at her companion. Yeah, nobody knew that, to her, Eric was so much more than a grieving family member.

They stepped into the September morning and walked to the end of the sidewalk near the parking lot. "Where's your car?"

Eric aimed the key fob at a gunmetal-gray Jeep Wrangler near the end of the first row and pressed the button.

The world exploded.

Eric dived, dragging Morgan down and instinctively rolling her beneath him. Gravel and dirt rained around them.

His ears rang, the initial shock of sound nearly blinding him. He fought to recover his senses, to remember this was Arizona, not overseas. This was safe ground.

Or what should be safe ground. He reached for his hip. No pistol. It was secured in his rental vehicle.

As the blast echoed away, he sat up and tucked Morgan behind him. A handful of people in the parking lot emerged from behind vehicles, pale and shaken.

Rangers rushed from every direction. They called orders and herded frightened visitors to safety.

No one seemed to be injured, although everyone was shaken.

It was likely a prank, but the explosion had been too loud to be fireworks or a soda-bottle bomb. It didn't matter. The entire government would descend soon, no matter how small the device.

"You okay?" He pivoted and reached for her, needing to reassure himself she was safe.

Morgan was pale. Too pale. Her deep brown eyes found the source of the explosion and she locked her gaze onto the smoking trash can. She might be present, but her mind was clearly somewhere else.

Eric had seen it in too many soldiers, when post-traumatic stress disorder and memories knocked them out of the present and into a past they refused to talk about.

Morgan was rattled, but not by what was happening in the moment. Something else haunted her.

Something much worse.

"Hey." Forgetting everything around them, Eric cradled her chin in his palms. His fingers lay across her cheek, over faint scars he had noticed years ago. Scars she'd never explained.

Pieces clicked into place. Sometime, somewhere, something had literally exploded in Morgan's face. Every piece of his heart that had ever loved her had to let her know she was safe.

Had to protect her. She might not be his any longer, but he would never let anything hurt her. "Morgan, it's me. It's Eric. You're safe. It's okay. It's really okay."

Her eyes shifted and narrowed as she searched his

face. She blinked rapidly and jerked her chin, tearing her gaze from his and ripping his hands from her face.

As though a switch flipped, the Morgan who'd vanished regained her park ranger bravado. She was on her feet, hand resting on the pistol at her hip, scanning the area. "What happened? Is everyone okay?" Her voice trembled, but anyone who didn't know her would likely miss it.

"Everyone seems to be fine." Eric urged her inside to safety, but she jerked away.

"I've got this. Get into the building and wait for instructions." She was already walking away, holding a hand out toward a group huddled in front of the wood-and-glass building, waving them toward the lobby. "I mean it, Eric."

Sure she did. He'd been wrong to treat her like a weak female in need of protection. She was competent and trained.

But she still needed someone to watch her back.

Eric dogged Morgan's footsteps into the lobby and stood to the side while the other park rangers took inventory of visitors, calmed frightened tourists and secured the area around the blast zone.

More Park Service employees arrived, clogging the space.

Eric's mind whirled, analyzing postures and gestures in the mass of people. Any one of them could have detonated the trash can as part of a larger plan to gather everyone into one place and then cause even worse damage.

Across the room near the service counters, Morgan engaged in a serious conversation with an older ranger, but her eyes scanned the room, a deep crease etched into her forehead. She was likely doing the same thing Eric was, evaluating the threat level.

Easing around a mother and her three teenage children, he made his way to Morgan's side.

The other ranger, Towbridge by his name tag, was speaking. "Investigative Services is coming in. Given the other incidents we've had recently, we're looking at a wide-scope investigation."

Morgan stood with her back to the wall, a defensive stance if Eric had ever seen one. "Will this affect my leave?"

"No." Towbridge shook his head as his phone buzzed. He reached for the device. "You're probably safer in the backcountry. Just be careful. Maybe reconsider going alone." Pulling the phone to his ear, he stepped away.

With a curt nod, Morgan turned and gasped as she saw Eric at her elbow. "How long have you been standing there?"

"Long enough. What *other incidents*?"

Her stare was guarded, her expression tense. With a glance to make sure no one was near, she lowered her voice. "There have been a handful of attacks on rangers in some of the isolated public areas of the park."

"So this could be an escalation, a threat of something bigger to come?"

The lines around her mouth tightened, and she flicked another glance at the crowd. "This could be as simple as fireworks and a bored teenager—"

"It was bigger than fireworks."

Morgan brushed past him, headed for a knot of people near the door. "You were here at the time of the blast. Investigators will want to talk to you as well as everyone else here. After you're released, pack and get some sleep. Meet me in the morning." She walked away. "You and I are done here."

TWO

Thunder echoed through the canyon, rolling from seemingly a thousand directions at once, a wave of sound that chilled Morgan from the inside out. Sure, it had been years since she left the city and started working as a backcountry law enforcement ranger, years since the bombing that had shattered lives and mangled her emotions...

Although the investigation had determined that the explosion three days earlier had been nothing more than fireworks, it had done more than rattle fragile nerves. It had thrown her into a time warp, from a trash can at the Grand Canyon to a backpack in a crowded concert venue...

Morgan's fingers traced the faint scars on her cheek and shuddered from the memories as a quick crack of thunder echoed against the canyon walls.

Morgan widened her stance and stared at the sky, anchoring herself in her surroundings as she forced herself to slowly inhale the warm canyon air. The narrow animal path before her, blue sky above her, darkening clouds to the northwest... Scrub brush and a few small tamarisk trees growing taller as they made the descent toward Lava Creek, the same route Eric and Hannah had traveled two weeks earlier.

She wasn't a rookie cop pulling security. She wasn't in San Diego. Nothing was exploding. She was below the rim with the man she used to love, the man whose sister was missing.

During an approaching thunderstorm.

But it couldn't shake her. She wouldn't let it. No matter what her past said, she would not be a coward.

Eric didn't seem to notice she'd stopped. He trudged ahead, watching the narrow animal path. They'd started day three making the seven-hundred-foot descent to Awatubi, then ascending to Awatubi-Sixtymile Saddle. Morgan hadn't made the trek in a while, and memory didn't come close to the view of multicolored rock as far as they could see.

There was no telling where Eric's head had been there. Probably remembering the last time he'd stood in the same spot, with his sister safely at his side. Morgan had nearly reached for his hand, but it was both too late and too soon. Instead, she'd offered him silent support until he'd moved forward without a word.

In fact, he hadn't said much of anything beyond, "loose rock" or "narrow foothold" since they'd hit the trail what felt like weeks ago.

Now they were on a narrow, rocky path, descending the east fork of Carbon Creek, which ran nearly dry. They'd end the day at Lava Creek, where Hannah had disappeared. Starting tomorrow morning, they'd be completely off the trail.

In the middle of the wilderness, Morgan was able to breathe for the first time since the trash can detonated. She was safe out here. No crowds. No bombs. Just scrub trees and rock and sky.

And the wrath of nature.

She glanced at the sky, tried to guess the distance of

the darkening clouds rolling in from the northwest, then calculated how long it would take to reach shelter. They were exposed in their current location.

"You thinking we need to find somewhere to shelter?" Eric's voice sliced into her thoughts. "I've been keeping an eye on it. Lightning's visible."

"If I've got a satellite phone signal, I'll call and see what we can get to quickly." She tugged out her phone. Depending on sky view, it could be tricky, but this time there was a connection and she dialed for a weather update. "How long before the storm hits? Any shelter near me?"

Ranger Seth Hanson at the station could access the information on his computer faster and more accurately than she could on a map, which gave elevations but not clefts and hollows in the rock.

The phone crackled, a sure sign she was pushing the limits. "From your location, about two hundred yards to the south. You should find cover there in a small cave. You're a good half hour from anything more substantial, and I don't think you're going to beat the storm to Lava. Watch you don't run into a rattler nest."

"Or rock squirrels."

The phone crackled over a rough connection. "Or rock squirrels. I'd shelter quick. Based on radar, the storm's going to rage for a while. Good thing you're not headed for the river. It's running high. Could be flash flooding, and there's talk of closing it to rafters. And stay safe. Too much weird stuff going on around here lately."

"Roger." She relayed the cave's location to Eric, then glanced at the sky, barely registering the ever-darkening clouds. Hannah was missing, and someone was coming at rangers. There were darker things at work in the world, things she didn't like to think about. It was the reason she'd chosen the solitary life of the backcountry.

"Is Larson in earshot?"

Morgan glanced at Eric, who had walked farther down the trail. She pressed the radio phone tighter to her ear anyway. "No."

"Think after this trek he'll finally accept we've moved from rescue to recovery?"

Morgan watched Eric scan the sky. There was no way he'd abandon the search for Hannah. Not until he had definitive proof all hope was lost. "Would you?"

"No. Stay safe. Out."

Tucking the phone away, Morgan made her way to Eric and relayed the latest. She followed him as he set his sights down the faint trail.

Despite what Hanson had said, Eric hadn't lost hope, and neither had Morgan. After all, a lost hiker in Hawaii had survived two weeks in harsh terrain and was found because her family refused to abandon the search. Maybe…

Maybe was a huge word.

Thunder ricocheted and Morgan stiffened but pushed forward. *Too many years, Morgan. You have to get over it. You can't be a coward forever.* Especially not in front of Eric.

Ahead of her, Eric ducked into a small opening in the rock, the cave Hanson had indicated. He stepped out with a rare ghost of a smile when Morgan approached. It did something to his eyes that almost made her retreat in shock. He was a handsome man on any given day, but with a lately unseen spark of life he was…more. A whole lot more.

He was the man she'd once fallen in love with.

Morgan closed her eyes, willing her past and her present to separate. She was a ranger helping a man search for his sister. The relief in his expression had to be because they were on the trail, moving forward, nearing the spot where they could begin the search for Hannah in earnest.

Eric's gaze flicked to hers, then to the northwest, where the storm shouted its presence again, louder as it closed in. "You know anything about the pizza I ordered, Dunham? I found out a while back you can get anything delivered by those car services if you pay enough. Figured I'd see if anyone was game for a big tip."

Wow. Humor, too. He was either ready to search or the heat had gotten to him. "Sure. Hanson's sending a helicopter with a large triple pepperoni, but the tip's going to be steep."

"It would be worth it. I've been craving a pizza since about two o'clock yesterday afternoon." He dragged a hand across days-old scruff along his cheek, then nodded to the sky. "I have no idea why pizza, but there you go." He surveyed the sky once more, then swept his hand to the side. "I made a quick scan. There are no bobcats or snakes. We should be safe in—"

A crack, close, as strange thunder bounced jagged off the canyon. The rock by Eric's head exploded, sending shards flying, striking pain along Morgan's cheek.

Familiar pain. Shrapnel. Screams.

Morgan froze and fought to stay in the now. They were in the canyon. Alone. There was no way—

Another crack and Eric shoved her into the cave. "Shooter!"

Another shot showered rocks, dust and dirt over them as Eric shoved Morgan deeper into the cave. She stumbled and he muscled all of his weight behind her, urging her forward.

Had someone really fired on them?

Inside the shelter of the shallow crevice, he bent forward and caught his breath, heart pounding as the adrenaline flooded his system.

Morgan regained her footing and faced the entrance, weapon drawn and steady in both hands, by her thigh.

Just like him. He didn't even remember drawing the pistol from its holster.

Pulling her attention from the entrance long enough to glance at him, Morgan said, "Tell me we were struck by lightning. Twice."

"Three times. I'm certain lightning doesn't work that way." No, he knew gunfire when he heard it, knew the whip crack of a rifle. The sound was different echoing through the Grand Canyon than it was flying across the mountains of Afghanistan, but it was the same retort, different tone. "Pretty sure it was a rifle. And a fair shot, too." He tipped his head toward the entrance. "Quick guess based on the way it hit, I'd have to say the bullet came from the rim on the far side."

"High-powered rifle."

"Possibly a sniper." Based on his calculations as they'd hiked, the distance was about two miles. Trajectory would help with travel, but whoever had fired was well practiced. Few rifles in the world could travel the distance with force. Even fewer marksmen could shoot with that sort of accuracy. Whatever had happened out there, it was no accident. While the chance they were being targeted was slim to none, he'd learned on more than one mission to plan for the worst and pray for the best. *Worst* right now involved being pinned in a cave with only one way out and no way to survey the world beyond.

Morgan pulled her phone from its spot on her pack. "If

somebody's taking shots at hikers in the area, we need to get a helicopter in the air and eyes high. Fast. Before they find cover."

A loud crash roared through the canyon, echoing over and over along the walls, the noise eerie and unfamiliar. He could live here a hundred years and never get used to the tone of thunder in the canyon.

The sound following chilled his blood more, though. Rain. Torrential rain driving toward them with a wall of water. Rain would obliterate any signs of Hannah and keep them trapped inside this crevice. "No help coming till this storm passes. And your sat phone won't get a signal with this cloud cover."

"We've got a while in this mess, according to my last call."

Eric ventured to the entrance, wind-whipped droplets cooling skin still heated from their trek deeper into the canyon. Two weeks ago following this same route with Hannah, he'd reveled in the exercise and the view. But this time his sister was missing. And now someone was taking potshots at tourists.

What if she wasn't lost? What if someone had… "No."

"No, what?" Morgan stepped closer, holstering her sidearm.

"Nothing." He hadn't realized he'd spoken out loud. The thought of Hannah lost and suffering was bad enough. The thought of her bleeding out because some psychopath got his jollies firing a sniper rifle at unsuspecting hikers…

He was going to be sick. Eric drew in deep gulps of the cooling air. He couldn't. He wouldn't. He had to stay strong if he was going to find Hannah alive.

Because she had to still be alive, and it was his job to rescue her.

He couldn't think about negative possibilities while he was tucked in a cave, hunkered down and hiding from Mother Nature and a possible killer. "If our friend out there decided to pursue and approach our location, how long would it take?" He couldn't take his eyes off the rain falling outside, the torrent so hard it obscured everything beyond three feet in front of him. That meant flash flooding. Which meant more danger to Hannah if she was caught in the elements.

"Assuming we're truly a target and they're foolish enough to try… And assuming they're on foot and don't have a helicopter… Several hours if you're right about the distance. It's not level ground. We're safe in here for now."

Eric willed his shoulders to relax and holstered his weapon, then faced Morgan for the first time. A thin rivulet of blood ran down her cheek from a small gash, likely where rock shrapnel had nicked her. His hand lifted to brush it off, but he simply awkwardly pointed. Contact would be out of bounds for both of them. It had been too long since he'd felt the soft skin of her cheek beneath his touch. "You got… You're bleeding."

In the bluish light flowing into their shallow shelter, the color drained from her face, highlighting the red streak of blood that flowed over the faint scars on her cheek. Her expression froze the way it had in the aftermath of the explosion, her eyes cast in the same faraway look.

Morgan wasn't afraid of blood, so Eric solidified the belief something had happened in her past.

Those scars she refused to talk about… Maybe before he met her? What had sent her to the backcountry and kept her there? How had he missed it during their brief marriage?

No matter. He could appreciate the need to run. It haunted him most nights as he lay awake remembering too much.

Eric started to reach for her again, to treat her the way he used to in their too-brief time together and pull her closer for comfort, but his gut stopped him. She was emotionally and physically tougher than anyone he knew. If he was in her shoes, he'd resent the "help." Instead, he stepped away a couple of feet to give her some space, to let her get her bearings. He pulled a small camp lantern from his pack and lit it, providing illumination in the semidarkness. It wasn't a deep recess, running back into the side of the canyon about ten feet, but it was enough to keep them dry and out of the range of lightning…or bullets.

Outside, the wind kicked up and the rain poured impossibly harder, sending a wave of damp air into their shelter.

He turned to Morgan. If she wasn't back to normal in about two minutes, he'd—

"I've got a first aid kit in my pack. It's… I'm sure it's nothing." A slight tremble in her voice said otherwise, but she was in motion and had slid the huge pack from her back before he could comment. As she withdrew a small white box from its pouch, her fingers fumbled and the kit clattered to the cave's rock floor. Morgan planted her hands on her knees and stared at the side wall of the cave, determination tightening her jaw and drawing a deep V between her eyes.

This wasn't fear. This was remembrance. The tension waving off her spoke to Eric's memories and struggles. Despite his earlier resolve, he couldn't let her do this alone. She'd stood beside him in the wake of his parents' deaths, had comforted him when no one else could… Was even now sacrificing her personal time to search for Hannah.

Crouching beside Morgan, Eric popped the latch on the first aid kit and dug out an alcohol wipe and a small bandage. He snapped on a thin pair of gloves to keep his trail-dusted fingers from adding an infection to the mix.

At the snap, she seemed to return to reality and cut her eyes sideways at him. "You doing surgery?"

"Only if there's really a pizza on the way. Otherwise, you get field medicine."

Arching an eyebrow, she held out her hand, palm up. "I can slap a bandage on my own face."

"But you can't tell if you need stitches, can you?" With a gentle hand, he grasped her chin and turned her cheek toward the light.

She yielded.

Surprising. He'd expected more resistance. For the briefest moment, he was caught in brown eyes that crossed the years to the time when they belonged to each other.

But that time wasn't now.

Eric forced his attention to the job at hand. Tearing open the alcohol wipe, he scanned the wound before going to work. It was merely a nick, but it sliced about half an inch across the field of smaller scars on her cheek.

He ran his thumb along the small dimples, barely visible unless someone was close enough to… Well, to kiss her. That was how he'd noticed them the first time, how he'd been led to ask her about them. Because he'd been close enough to kiss her. In all the years since, he'd honestly never imagined he'd be this close to her again.

"Is it so bad you're contemplating a cheek amputation?"

Eric cleared his throat, pulled his fingers from her cheek, then gently wiped the area with the alcohol pad.

Though she'd cracked a joke, the tightness in Morgan's voice and in her facial muscles betrayed her anxiety.

Still, he'd play along. "So, Ranger Dunham. What brings you to my clinic? The fabulous online reviews? The heroic tales of my cheek-doctoring skills?"

She winced as the alcohol did its work. "I was told you have pizza."

He actually snorted. Her sense of humor ran deeper than he remembered. Sweet. "Well, the driver's late. No tip when they get here." As Eric opened the bandage, he paused to stare at the small figures dotting the white surface.

"You carry princess bandages in the backcountry?"

"What can I say? I'm whimsical."

"Whimsical." He kept his voice flat, though a smile tugged the corners of his mouth. It felt good to be amused, to think about something else after long days and nights of driven fear over Hannah.

Even if that something was his ex-wife.

Dude, he was in so much trouble.

Thunder roared, closer as the storm intensified.

Morgan jumped, grasping for the wall with her hand.

"What's scaring you?" The words were out before he could stop them, born of a kindred fear that drove him to help her.

The friendliness in her eyes hardened and she shoved herself upward, pacing to the cave's entrance. "Nothing scares me. You need to be less concerned about me and more concerned with finding a way to fight Mother Nature and to outwit someone who's out there with a gun."

Out there with a gun…and possibly with his sister.

THREE

Eric turned from the cave's entrance and reached for his backpack. "If this goes on much longer, I'm heading out anyway."

Morgan's head snapped up. It was the first time he'd spoken since he'd come awfully close to guessing her secrets, seeing her fear. She shook off her shame.

Was he kidding? Sure, he'd been stubborn from the start—it had been one of the many things working against their marriage—but to take his life into his own hands on a nearly invisible trail? The turnoff to Lava Creek and Still Spring was tough to find on a clear day, let alone in the mess falling outside. "Absolutely not."

"My sister is out there." His voice was hard, determined. The cheerful gleam that lit his eyes earlier had hardened into a glint as cold as mid-January. "She's out there in this. With a—" He jabbed a finger toward the cave's entrance and, presumably, to the other side of the canyon. Gone was the gentle touch that had tended her wound. Gone was the knowing look that said he understood more than she wanted him to.

She was dealing with the Eric Larson who'd bucked the National Park Service at every turn in the search for his sister, who'd been unwilling to bend his life for their marriage...

She hadn't yielded either.

Morgan couldn't fault him for the emotion concerning Hannah, but she couldn't let him walk into certain death either. "You breaking an arm or a leg out here isn't going to help her. It will only get you a quick ride out with an air evacuation." She held up a hand before he could speak. "Same if you get shot."

"The rain gives me cover."

"The rain washes out what little trail there is. There are more dangerous things in the canyon than humans. Chances are we're looking at a hunter with bad eyesight." No matter what they'd discussed earlier, it had to be that. Why would someone wait for days in volatile weather for the possibility a ranger or a hiker would happen by?

"We both know not. Hunters aren't packing that kind of firepower. A hunter wouldn't fire at a trophy he can't get to before it's wrecked in the rain." He kicked a rock that disappeared into the downpour.

"The only way a sniper makes sense is if one of us is the target."

Eric dropped away from the cave entrance, though he kept a wary eye on the rain. "A bomb exploded at the ranger station. There have been multiple attacks on rangers lately. It's possible someone has a grudge against the Park Service and has been waiting out here for a back-country patrol or—"

"Or they could be waiting for you."

"That's even more far-fetched."

Not even three full days on the trail and they were fighting like two-year-olds.

Morgan flinched as lightning struck nearby, the crash

a rolling freight train as it bounced off the rock face. The odds of being struck were one in seven hundred thousand. A few hours away in Vegas, people gambled on worse. Morgan rested her palm on the grip of her pistol and tapped her finger against the holster. "Is there any reason someone would want to come after you?"

"That's insane."

"Enlighten me. It's not exactly like we have a Broadway show in here to entertain us. Might as well exercise our imaginations."

"You always did like a good musical." His smile was quick, a flash like the lightning outside, gone so fast she wasn't even sure it'd been real.

Morgan shuddered the sensation away. Eric Larson was a man searching desperately for his sister. A man who had already proved his career didn't dovetail with building a relationship…ever.

This was strictly professional.

"Fine. I'll play along. If this is truly targeted, it's a whole lot more likely we're dealing with a disgruntled former government employee who's out to make a point. And if that's the case, the person we need to be worried about protecting is you." Eric returned to his position beside her. "Even discounting the recent attacks, I know the statistics. I know law enforcement rangers are way more likely to be assaulted than their counterparts in local law enforcement, FBI and other investigative services. I know there are missing-ranger cold cases out there. I know—"

"How?"

"Because I looked into the job. And for eight years I've had a Google alert set for…" He inhaled deeply and turned away. "Let's say I've been following the situation."

I've been looking out for you. The unspoken words

were clear in the still air. He'd been watching and worrying from a distance the same way she had. Why?

Likely the same reason she'd held her breath and said a prayer every Sunday night as she typed his name into the search box, praying she'd never be confronted with a flag-backed photo announcing his death.

She opened her mouth to commiserate, to rebuild a bond, then stopped. This wasn't a conversation they should be having, especially not in their current situation. The rain slacked off, and the thunder grew distant as the wind screamed with less force. "I think we need to decide on our next move. I should have a signal soon and be able to call in. The best thing to do is to wait for an aircraft to get a line of sight on the other side of the canyon so we can get boots on the ground to investigate. We'll get to safety until the shooter's in custody. I'll—"

"No." His voice was emphatic and hard. "I'm not walking away when my sister is out there. You can do what you want, but I'm heading straight to Lava Creek like we planned." He glanced at the almost nonexistent rain, hefted his pack and moved to shoulder past her. "You do whatever you want. You owe me nothing."

"Eric, wait." Her hand on his biceps stopped his determined forward motion. "You're not going alone. The Park Service put conditions on you being allowed out here. Like it or not, you're stuck with me. If something happens to you…"

What she didn't say slumped his shoulders. *If something happens to you, Hannah is lost forever.* Eric's muscles tightened. "Fine, but I call the—"

"No, I call the shots, or I make one call to have your backcountry pass revoked and you hauled out of here as fast as I can get an aircraft inbound. Are we clear?"

Eric fixed his eyes on the far side of the canyon, visible as the storm moved on.

"Eric, listen..." Morgan took a deep breath and went where neither of them had yet dared. "You know you can trust me, but I need to be able to trust I won't turn around and find out you've hightailed it out on your own."

His index finger worked double time on his thigh. Truth was, he was in no position to refuse her help and they both knew it.

"Agreed."

One battle down. "I'll try to get a signal once the cloud cover clears, but if one shot gets fired when we step out of here, then we shelter in place and wait for backup. I'm not risking our lives to a trigger-happy sharpshooter or a hunter with zero common sense."

Eric nodded but remained silent, focused on outside the cave.

There was no doubt what he was doing. Considering their situation, Morgan was certain he searched for signs someone was watching through a rifle scope.

The sun was lower than Morgan wanted it to be by the time they reached Lava Creek, the shadows long but the air a good twenty degrees warmer than it had been at higher elevations. The creek ran as more than the usual trickle after the storms, enough to splash away the heat of the day but not enough to be worrisome. Cottonwood trees around the creek provided shade and shelter from anyone who might take a potshot from above.

Most people who'd never been in the backcountry pictured the canyon as a claustrophobic channel with steep walls to the sky. While that was true of some spots, this location offered a wide expanse of sky.

Morgan's body ached from three days of hiking, and her temples throbbed with stress. Every muscle had been tight since they left the crevice, tensed from the wait for a bullet to pierce her skin. Half of her was certain the shooter had already fled while the other half could feel him watching from some hideaway. She wanted to believe it was a one-off, a hunting accident, a poacher who pulled the trigger without thinking… Oh, how she had spent the majority of the hike praying it was so. Anything else was unthinkable.

Worse, while the rain had cleared, the clouds had never lifted, rendering the satellite phone unusable. No help was on the way.

Eric stalked her footsteps about eight feet behind, the same space he'd occupied the entire hike. She hadn't dared to look at him, but from the sound of a couple of his stumbles, he'd been more intent on searching for a muzzle flash on the rim than he had been on dogging her footsteps.

They had an unspoken agreement. She kept an eye on the trail, and he kept an eye on the rocky rim above them.

Under the coverage of a cottonwood tree, Morgan slid her pack to the ground and tilted her head side to side to roll away some of the tension. "Here looks good. We've got the creek to replenish water, and we're sheltered from anything above." They'd have to draw water and let it sit for a few hours before they could purify it, but they had time.

She eyed Eric. Would he chafe at stopping while it was still daylight? Especially here, where Hannah had vanished?

Eric shifted his gaze from the sky to the ground, sweeping back and forth. He was probably making sure none of the six species of rattlesnakes in the canyon was lying in wait. While all of the snakes she'd ever seen had slithered off rather than confront her, the creatures were still her least favorite thing about backcountry patrols.

He sniffed and aimed a finger up the creek. "You know this is where…"

"I know." It wasn't rattlesnakes that had him restless. It was memories. Guilt. Grief. If only she knew what to say to make it better, but there was nothing. Not as long as Hannah Larson seemed to have vanished from the planet.

Eric dropped his pack and settled beside it with his back against the base of a tree, then took a long draw from his insulated water bottle. His expression shifted as though he'd made a decision. "What's the plan for dinner since our pizza never arrived?"

"I'm thinking tonight will be a freeze-dried favorite. You?" They hadn't discussed communal dinners, but it wouldn't hurt if they were careful about rationing. While there were a few caches of field rations stashed along some of the backcountry routes, running out of food below the rim was a quick path to trouble. For the past two nights, they'd silently eaten their own meals, but if he was willing to be social… "We can see if we have anything that complements each other."

Ooh. That was probably the wrong way to word it.

Eric didn't bat an eye. "I've got pretty much the same as you. Oh, and some kind of homemade peanut butter protein bars I've been saving. A lady at the ranger station knew who I was and gave them to me before I headed out. She was waiting when I dropped off the Jeep and told me she'd been praying for Hannah."

"You're going to eat food a stranger handed you?" Call her overly cautious and maybe a little scared, but she'd developed a distrust of strangers over her years as a law enforcement officer. There were too many people in this world willing to harm others. It was one of the reasons she'd taken this job in the backcountry, where the most she had to worry about was wild animals. Including snakes, of course.

Until today.

"She was a volunteer. One of the rangers at the station vouched for her. Wish I could remember her name."

Wait. Homemade peanut butter bars? Morgan smiled. The gift-bearing lady was no stranger. "A little shorter than me? In her seventies? Big eyes and a bigger smile?"

"Yep."

"Angel Campos. She volunteers quite a bit, was probably on the initial search for Hannah. She's retired from the Park Service but still shows up pretty faithfully." Morgan settled to the ground and leaned against her pack, her legs finally realizing they'd stopped for the day and refusing to move any farther until she rested. "Angel is named well. If she says she's praying for Hannah, then it's more than a quick prayer while she's walking out the door. She's been on her face on the floor all night, asking God to watch out for your sister." Angel held legendary status among the rangers for her selflessness, going above and beyond even in her retired years.

Her retired years. She'd been around a long time. Had been working at the park even before Morgan was assigned. Which meant… "Eric, she didn't happen to find you. She's probably been keeping tabs on you. I doubt you remember, but she was likely involved in the search for your parents when they disappeared on the river."

"Hmm." He stared into the distance, probably seeing the past more than the rocks and creek in front of him.

"She learned you planned to head out and made a point to be there. She was probably awake in the dark hours to cook and pray for you."

Clearing his throat, Eric looked across at her. "They were still warm when she handed them to me."

"I'll guarantee there's a smaller bag inside with a verse on it. That's how Angel operates."

Eric eyed her, one eyebrow raised and his lips pursed in thought. "You know I have to look right now, don't you?"

"I expected no less." On day one of the hike, he'd shared that he'd become a Christian after their divorce. She'd seen enough this week to know Eric Larson walked what he talked... And he talked what he walked.

Unzipping a side pouch on his pack, he pulled out a bag of crushed peanut butter bars, shoved a bite into his mouth, then pulled out a second smaller zip-top bag from the inside. He tossed her the snack, then held up his prize. "You were right." He thumbed crumbs from the side of the bag, stuck his thumb in his mouth to keep from wasting the homemade goodness, then read the verse through the clear plastic.

Morgan tried not to stare, but the way his expression changed from grief to peace to awe riveted her. His eyes, too rich of a brown to be real, almost seemed to darken as he read.

He dragged his hand across his mouth, then rummaged through his bag and pulled out a water purification kit. "We need water. I'll be back." He dropped the plastic-wrapped message in her lap as he passed, then disappeared toward the creek.

FOUR

I will lift up mine eyes unto the hills, from whence cometh my help. My help cometh from the Lord, which made heaven and earth. He will not suffer thy foot to be moved; he that keeps thee will not slumber.

The first three verses of Psalm 121. King James Version. Eric turned onto his back in the lightweight sleeping bag and stared at the stars through the branches of a cottonwood tree. He should be sleeping while Morgan kept watch, getting ready for their shift change at two, but he couldn't. He was...floored. Broken.

What was that word his great-grandmother had been so fond of using? *Gobsmacked.*

He was gobsmacked. Or maybe more appropriately, God-smacked.

He'd smile if the situation wasn't so mind-blowing. He knew those verses by heart straight out of the King James Version. Hannah had gone to the military surplus store and had a patch made before his first deployment, one he'd carried with him ever since. Even now, the well-worn scrap of fabric lay tucked into the top flap of his backpack.

The same words he'd received from a stranger who

had not only searched for Hannah but was doing some serious praying on her behalf, as well.

He hadn't discovered it night one or night two on the trail... But on night three. In the exact spot where Hannah had vanished, where he needed it most.

Eric dragged both hands down his face, palms scraping against stubble. Since he'd read Angel's message, peace reigned, almost as though God was telling him it would be okay, no matter what the circumstances said.

With all of his heart, Eric wanted to believe his sister was alive. His mind knew the chances were slim. Even without flooding rains, Hannah was two weeks in the wild without provisions.

Eric sat up, sleeping bag pooling at his waist. No. Absolutely not. He couldn't abandon her. Everyone else had. *Recovery* had become the byword, but he'd find her. He'd bring her home again.

This was the thing he'd wrestled with for months as he embraced the suck in Afghanistan and prayed to make it home with his buddies in one piece. Was it time to separate from the army? Time to move home and be closer to Hannah so she wouldn't have to worry about losing him, too?

He tried to close his eyes and breathe deeply but uneasiness crept in and stole his rest. It was like those times overseas, moments before the bad guys pulled something terrible. Those weird, back-of-his-mind feelings that said something was wrong, even when logic said there was nothing to worry about.

The day's events had him too charged, too tightly wound to rest.

With a huff, he kicked off the sleeping bag. Since he was awake, he might as well stand watch and let Morgan rest.

A thud and a scrape drifted from the creek.

Eric scrambled to his feet and ran before he could fully process the sound. Maybe it was simply nature being nature, a bobcat pouncing on prey, anything other than Morgan in danger. He didn't dare call out to her, not when a stranger might be out there.

Sharp rocks and twigs jabbed at his bare feet as he rushed to the creek's edge, where Morgan stood watch. Thick clouds hid the moon. Nothing moved except the creek, whose waters trickled over rocks loud enough to dampen every other sound.

Morgan's water bottle was there, but she was gone.

So much like Hannah.

Eric jerked his head from side to side, trying to see, trying to hear. He should have brought a flashlight, but—

A small sound behind him and the world vanished as something covered his head. Felt like canvas. A force pulled the rough material against his face and dragged him backward.

Dark. Too dark.

Eric fought with every evasive maneuver he knew, but the darkness and lack of air muddied his mind. His body ached. His lungs screamed for air. It was too hard to tell if the darkness was from without or within as his brain screamed for oxygen that came in thin, hot wisps.

Not enough.

Eric shoved an elbow backward and made contact, but the jab was weak. He struggled against growing darkness.

He was slipping. Slipping…

It was too quiet.

Morgan had been antsy since Eric disappeared to his sleeping bag, the silence around the creek too heavy.

Nothing moved. No creatures had anything to say. Restless, she'd walked to the bend in the creek, listening, searching...

It wasn't right. Something always scurried in the darkness, particularly near water. Yet for the past half hour, the only sound had been the creek trickling over rocks.

Thick clouds obscured the moon, but her night vision had adjusted after hours in the darkness and afforded her enough sight to keep her flashlight off. Turning it on would give away their position if anyone was looking for them.

Highly unlikely, but still...

Glancing at her watch, she headed toward the makeshift campsite under the cottonwoods. It was close to time to wake Eric for his watch, but it seemed cruel to do so. It was likely she wouldn't sleep anyway, not when all she could envision was a rifle-toting shadow around every corner.

Rocks crunched under her feet as she neared the spot where she'd left her water bottle, but another sound layered over everything else.

Shuffling. A sharp grunt. A muffled shout.

Morgan reached for her pistol as she ran toward the campsite.

Two men wrestled in the semidarkness, one hooding another's head with what looked to be a small backpack.

Two men. Fighting. One had to be Eric, but from a distance it was impossible to distinguish the tangled figures.

Drawing her sidearm, she held it aimed at the ground. Morgan edged closer as quickly as she dared, hoping to keep the element of surprise, heart pounding.

The man whose face was covered dropped to his knees, his energy clearly waning. For the first time, she got a view of the assailant's shape in the near darkness and it wasn't Eric. He was too short, too slight.

Morgan bolted into action, raising her weapon. "Park Service! Let him go!"

The world froze. The fighting hesitated, then Eric's attacker shoved him in a tumble toward the creek and ran north into the scattering of trees.

Morgan took two steps in pursuit but stopped. Running headlong into the night would be foolish. No light, no trail, no idea who was out there or what they were capable of.

And Eric nearly motionless by the creek…

She skidded to her knees beside him, then eased him to a sitting position and pulled the bag from his head.

He gulped in lungfuls of air and shook his head as if to clear it.

Morgan's fingers trailed his face, then down tight muscles in his neck, searching for damage. "You okay?"

"Shaky, but good." He pushed away, leveraging himself against the ground to stand.

Morgan rose with him. He was not fine. His hands shook and it was clear he'd been close to unconsciousness…if he hadn't been completely out.

He could have been killed while she was roaming the area instead of standing watch the way she should have. She'd missed all of the signs. Nothing had changed. She was a disgrace to her badge.

She was a ranger. Trained. Trusted. Better than allowing her "partner" to be sneak attacked in the night. "Eric, I'm calling for help as soon as the skies clear. You're not well."

"I'm fine. And we need to follow him." Eric straightened, wavered for a second, then seemed to get his bearings. He stared to the north, in the direction his attacker had fled. "I'm going after him."

"No way. He's got a decent head start, we don't know if he's armed and we can't use flashlights because they'd pinpoint our location."

Eric marched a few feet away, hands on hips, his back a solid wall. He was probably debating whether to listen. She was familiar with his stubbornness, his need for action.

Well, this time he was wrong. This time, he'd almost been killed.

Adrenaline robbed her strength. *He'd almost been killed.* Her knees threatened to go soft on her. If he'd died, it would have been her fault.

"Fine. I won't follow him. But you're not having me carted out of here like some wisp of nothing who can't get over thirty seconds without oxygen. I can hold my breath."

"You were nearly unconscious."

"I'm okay."

Morgan's jaw tightened. They could stand here and argue or they could take action. "Fine." She turned and strode toward their makeshift campsite and her pack. Maybe she'd be able to get a signal on the satellite phone, though the sky was obscured. "I'm still calling this in. The sooner we get other rangers on this, the faster they bring in whoever this guy is." Even if she managed to get a signal, it would be morning before a search could start, but Morgan didn't care. Her deepest hope was the guy didn't try again.

But something was wrong. If he was armed, he'd have shot Eric rather than try to suffocate him or drag him away. "Why the canvas bag?"

He stopped, staring toward the campsite as she stepped beside him. "What?"

"Assuming this is the same guy who fired on us earlier, why not kill you? Why waste the time trying to render you unconscious? Why struggle with you instead of taking you out?" In training and over her years in law enforcement, she'd learned small details were the most telling, and nonsensical things were important things.

She started walking, urging Eric forward. "We need to get out of here, get moving before he returns and brings friends with him."

Eric merely walked beside her and a half step ahead, probably aware she'd never let him take point in front of her.

Under the trees, Morgan stomped to her sleeping bag and reached for her pack, which she'd set by the opening.

It was gone.

Surely she was missing it.

But there was enough light to make out shapes in the area. She made a slow circuit, then faced Eric, stark realization taking hold. "My pack's missing."

All of her communication and survival gear were gone.

FIVE

Eric spun and jogged to where he'd been trying to rest. He tripped over the end of his sleeping bag and stopped.

No way. He turned in the same slow motion as Morgan. His backpack was gone, as well. How had someone gotten past them?

"He's not working alone." Morgan stepped closer, her voice grim. She held up a watertight bag. "Food was in the tree to protect it from animals and we have the water we filtered earlier, but…"

As she trailed off, Eric glanced toward the cottonwood about fifty feet from where he'd been lying before his anonymous attacker struck. The shadow of the pack that held his food and water filtration kit still hung there. They had food. They had water and the ability to purify more given enough time, but nothing else. No GPS, no maps, no communication.

In the literal middle of nowhere, they were completely cutoff and at the mercy of whoever was clearly trying to send them a deadly message. Eric's lungs burned with the reminder.

That wasn't the worst part. He'd lowered his guard, had failed to protect his sister and Morgan. If he'd been taken out tonight because he wasn't paying attention, there would be no one left to spearhead the search for Hannah... And there was no telling what a sadistic madman would do to Morgan in the backcountry with Eric out of the way.

"Eric?"

He scratched his stiff neck and turned to her. "Well, you wondered why they didn't try to kill us. Looks like they opted for the slow way."

Pinching the bridge of her nose, Morgan lifted her face to the clouds. She was either praying or trying to think of a way out of this. If the past was an indicator, she was praying.

"How long before they organize a search party for a missing ranger?"

"Communication can be spotty this far out, especially if the clouds hang on, and I'm technically on vacation. Still, they'll expect contact. I'd guess it will be about twenty-four hours before they worry." Morgan slowly lowered her head to meet his gaze. "I just realized something, though."

She was standing exceptionally close, so close he could make out her features, even in the semidarkness. He could feel her warmth. In spite of several days in the backcountry, the faintest scent of citrus still clung to her, probably shampoo or...

Eric took one step away. What kind of idiot was he, noticing such things right now? He cleared his throat. "Tell me you realized something good."

She gave a small shake of her head. "I was out there alone while you slept. No one came at me."

His gut twisted into freefall the same way it had when the call came about his parents' deaths, in the same way it had when he realized Hannah was really gone. "I'm the target." He watched Morgan pace toward her sleeping bag. "Unless taking me out would make you vulnerable? Someone could be preying on...on females." Nausea clinched his gut. Preying on his sister.

Morgan turned away and rolled up her gear with quick, jerky movements. Even from this distance in the faint dark, there was a tense anger about her motions, one he couldn't fault her for. Anger, pain and the edge of fear gnawed at him, too.

But there was no time to dwell on what felt like an unfolding horror movie. They had to get moving and conceal their location. Following her lead, he crafted a makeshift pack from his sleeping bag, then stowed his food inside.

If he kept moving, he couldn't think, couldn't imagine his sister in the hands of a madman.

I will lift up mine eyes unto the hills, from whence cometh my help. My help cometh from the Lord, which made heaven and earth. The words cycled over and over. Could he risk truly believing them? Because believing meant he couldn't help himself and Morgan or Hannah.

Only God could.

No. Eric was God's boots on the ground, and he had to keep moving or Hannah was lost forever.

Before he finished packing, Morgan was at his side, her bundled sleeping bag slung over her shoulder, hand resting on the grip of her pistol at her hip.

He'd stashed his gun in his pack before bedding down. With his pack gone, only one of them was armed, and if he had to guess, all Morgan had for ammunition was the bullets in her magazine. The bad news kept snowballing.

"I don't know if you're the target or if I am, and it doesn't matter. Our biggest priority is making an almost three-day hike out of here as quickly as possible, because without communication…" She sighed heavily and hefted her bag higher onto her shoulder. "You didn't happen to keep a flashlight in with your food did you?"

"Nope."

"Figures." She stepped slowly toward the river. "All I have is a small LED light, but using it is dangerous. We can hike a little ways along the creek edge, but we'll have to move slowly and try to retrace our steps. No telling where holes or critters are hiding. One wrong step, and we're in trouble. There's no way for me to carry you out of here, and I doubt you want to hike out with me on your back either."

With the ascents and descents they'd made over the past three days, the thought of one of them injured was more than he was ready to contemplate.

Morgan eyed the sky. To the northwest, stars began to peek out and the full moon brightened the sky. Light would be both a blessing and a curse.

Morgan made a slow turn and faced south, away from the direction they'd hiked for the past few days. "Actually, I have a better idea."

"I'm game for anything."

"Whoever is following expects us to retrace our steps and hike out. It will be a hard trek with only what we have left. We have no extra water and no time to wait for more to settle before we have to get moving. What if we do the unexpected?"

"Which is…?"

"We parallel the path you originally planned to take with Hannah and make our way to the Colorado. There's a cache with provisions where Lava Creek comes out. If the river isn't too high for it after all of the rains, we can flag down some rafters and hitch a ride or get a message out. Get more people searching, get some supplies, then return and resume our original search path. It will cost us a couple of days, but it might be our best option." She hefted her bag and started walking. "We'll have to stay out of sight and not right along the creek. It will take twice as long and be a tough slog, but it's doable."

He fell into step behind Morgan, watching her take step by methodical step along a nonexistent trail. Her head swiveled as she searched the ground in the ever-increasing moonlight, probably watching for snakes and hidden holes.

Eric exhaled and tore his eyes from her to watch the area around them. Turning away from their planned search route was harder than he expected, his muscles aching to continue the search for Hannah. But he had to follow Morgan and get to safety. They were in direr straits than she'd verbalized, with a long trek ahead of them and only one day's worth of water each. Any delay in getting to the river and neither they nor Hannah would make it out of the backcountry alive.

Adrenaline had long ago worn off, and the aftermath was not Morgan's friend.

They'd been walking for two hours at a century-old tortoise's pace. Every muscle ached. The gnawing anxiety of being trapped in the backcountry with a stalker and no way to call for help dogged every step. And Eric's steady breathing close on her boot heels layered the past over every thought.

What would life be like if he'd been willing to stay here with her? If she'd been willing to pack everything to go with him?

She rolled her shoulders and kept her eyes on the ground. *Focus.* It was her job to get them out of this alive, to lead them to the river and help.

Their nighttime journey was doubly tough when past memories clashed swords with present danger. They weren't alone out here. Someone was tailing them, toying with them. Every theory she came up with shattered under one question: Why keep them alive when killing them would be easier?

Somewhere nearby was a small cave with a barely visible opening etched into the rock face. It would offer them a place to rest and maybe to hide, at least until they could set off with more energy.

Morgan brushed her fingers across the grip of her Glock, taking a small measure of comfort from its weight at her side. The magazine held only fifteen rounds.

Fifteen rounds to protect them from dangerous animals… or dangerous humans.

A shove from behind pushed her forward another step.

"Why'd you stop?" Eric edged around to stand beside her.

She must have slowed, dragged by her thoughts. "We have to break soon. If we don't rest, we're never going to make it through this." She glanced around. "If I'm not totally missing my mark and walking in circles, there's a cave nearby. The bend in the creek back there is the landmark for it." She stepped closer to the rock face, searching for a shadow to indicate the entrance.

There. "It's a tight squeeze in, but that's in our favor."

They tromped the last hundred yards, turning sideways to slip into the darkness. Morgan produced her pocket flashlight, finally feeling she could use it without giving away their location. She swept the area. No animals. No spiders. No snakes. At least not in plain sight, and she sure wasn't going on the hunt for one.

She dropped her bedroll, tension easing for the first time in hours. For the moment, they were safe, hidden from view and hopefully out of harm's way. "I think we're clear."

Eric slid his makeshift pack from his shoulder, then settled to the ground beside it, rubbing his neck. He'd probably wrenched it during the attack. "Far as I could tell, nobody followed us. Tough to hear, but I didn't see anything suspicious."

Neither of them had seen anything at the campsite either. "I say we rest here and wait for daylight. Grab something to eat and keep going. The river's too muddy here to filter water from it, so we have to go with what we've got. Once we reach the river there's a cache with MREs and water so we won't have to wait hours to filter it." No ammo and no radio, but the knowledge that supplies lay ahead at least offered hope…even if the food was military rations.

"Mmm… MREs. Nothing like 'Mr. E' to make life better." Sarcasm laced Eric's voice, then he sat forward. "Maybe we'll get lucky and there'll be a chili mac. Not the greatest, but it has pound cake. And coffee."

"You know way too much about this."

"Hey, everybody has a favorite. I've seen guys almost come to blows over chow." He scratched the side of his nose and stared over her head as though he could see a memory there. "My last deployment, we had a guy who hated chicken. Hated it. Wouldn't touch the stuff. We'd been in the middle of nowhere forever, living off what was in our rucksacks, so MREs were an oasis in the desert. When we got them, every meal was chicken. Poor guy lived for two weeks on whatever nobody else wanted out of their chow."

Clearly, he was feeling relief at being tucked out of sight. Either that or this was a coping mechanism. Eric was talking about the past to keep from thinking too much about the present. She could appreciate the motivation behind the words.

He clearly loved the military. Knowing him and his constant drive for adventure, he'd seen and done it all. Morgan sank to the ground across from him, her weary muscles grateful for rest. "What made you want to be a soldier?" They'd never talked about it before. Maybe it was off-limits, too close to the thing that had kept them apart.

Maybe he wasn't the only one who'd rather talk about anything other than their current dire situation.

Eric didn't seem to notice her verbal faux pas. At least, he didn't react to it. He stretched out his legs and rocked his feet from side to side, probably working the kinks out of his ankles. "No fair. I asked you about rangering, years ago. You blocked me. Changed the subject. Complete—"

"Got it." He'd always been given to exaggeration. It was one of the things she'd fallen in love with. He could make her laugh when no one else could.

For the first time ever, she wanted to tell the truth and confess the fear that had driven her into the wild.

Maybe it was because he was no longer tied to her future. Maybe it was because there were no longer high stakes between them, and he couldn't call her a coward and then leave the way the man before him had. Maybe it was because he was hurting and scared over Hannah and she wanted to give him something.

Whatever the reason, she was about to tell him the story he'd asked her about so many times.

She was about to trust him.

SIX

Morgan crossed her arms over her stomach to hold in her emotions. If she told him the truth, that she'd failed in a thousand ways, it had to be a completely rational thing. She'd have to stand against the sting of judgment in his eyes when he realized she was, at her deepest core, more fear than anything else. "Where I've been is not a lighthearted frolic in the sunflowers. Just so you're forewarned."

"Because where I've been was oh so sunflower filled. Although, I can say I've seen my share of poppies in Afghanistan." He arched an eyebrow. "And it's nothing like *The Wizard of Oz*."

Oh my. It was a carbon copy of the look he'd given her the first time he'd kissed her. Half amused, half serious, all attention focused on her.

No. Too much had happened in their lives and in their shared history for him to look at her like that again.

Anxiety and hunger drove her spiking heart rate. That was all. "You remember I was a police officer for a year before I went to work for the Park Service and met you."

"In San Diego. You liked the open air better than the city."

"Sort of." If *I panic anytime I'm in a crowd* counted as open air.

Morgan dug her teeth into her lower lip. She wasn't really going to tell him the entire story, was she? It would change everything.

Then again, everything had already changed. "I had a friend who was opening a concert venue and in my off-hours I did some part-time work for him, helped him hire security staff, pulled some off-duty security for him."

"Friend or boyfriend?" Eric focused on relacing his boot, not looking at her.

"Does it matter?"

"No. I just wondered."

"Boyfriend." Although they'd talked about becoming more *someday*, Kevin had never been the kind to truly commit, and Morgan had known it all along. Every time she tried to walk away, though, he charmed her right back. Something about his lazy grin and those ocean-blue eyes.

Blue eyes that had grown so icy cold.

Morgan fought a shudder. It was hard enough to tell the story without bringing Kevin into it. "On opening night he has this local band come in, a group that had started to make a name for themselves in the Southwest, Absence Blockade."

"I remember them." Eric shifted and bent his knee to rest his elbow on it. "Used to listen to them when I was in high school. They were getting huge until the lead singer was killed when a…" His eyes caught hers, understanding drawing deep lines in his forehead. "When a bomb went off in a club in San Diego."

The carnage when a backpack near the stage detonated with a force that blasted out doors and killed ten people… The subsequent days of manhunt and fear with a bomber on the loose... No one on the outside could fully under-stand what it was like to hunt for a man who spent days taunting the police. What it was like to halt transportation and walk streets as silent as any ghost town, methodically searching for a killer who ultimately went out in a blaz-ing gun battle that killed a police officer and a firefighter.

For months afterward, the city had closed in on her. Even small crowds sucked the air from her lungs and ac-celerated her heart rate. Morgan had never known a panic attack before, but they came at her almost daily, usually when she was off duty and unarmed.

"We can summarize it by saying wide-open spaces and very few people became my friend. Leaving law enforcement didn't feel right, so I looked at the Park Service, went through training and was hired. A small park in the Virginia mountains was my first assignment. I was there for a year, and you pretty much know the rest." She shrugged. "Now I spend ten days patrolling land very few people have ever seen, taking in views most people can't even dream of. Basically hiding from the world and labeling it a good cause." Okay, had she seriously said that last part? Morgan dropped her head against the rock.

Eric didn't say anything for a long time.

The opposite of Kevin, who'd told her to get over it. He'd blamed her for not spotting a backpack no one else had seen either. He'd called her a weak coward.

Had ultimately walked away with the manager of his club, a woman who was tough, strong and unafraid. Ev-erything Morgan wasn't.

Everything Eric had made her feel like she could be again.

In his look there was a flash of the perfect harmony

that had once fueled their lives, back when she'd made him her everything.

When he finally spoke, his voice was low, almost as though the conversation was sacred to him and required a certain respect. "I've seen too many things happen in crowds, so I can understand completely what you're saying." He sniffed. "That's why gunshots don't make you flinch. It's not death. It's not bullets. It's the fear of missing something again. Of not seeing the backpack... Or the trash can. It's the out-of-control need to watch every move every single person around you makes. There's a drive that has nothing to do with self-preservation. It's rooted in the need to make sure everyone around you is safe. If you miss something..." He turned away, his profile sharp in the semidarkness. "If you miss something and somebody else pays the price, then you can't shake the feeling of failure." Eric's eyes were dark, shadowed by flashlight and emotion, and he studied the small opening through which they'd entered the cave. "I was in a Mexican restaurant once. Saw a guy reading a book about Charles Manson in the corner. Alone. He walked away from his table and left his briefcase beside his chair."

Morgan's heart beat faster thinking about it. The image in her mind was enough to make her want to run screaming deeper into the backcountry. "There's the dilemma... Do you raise the alarm and make a fool of yourself because maybe he's simply a guy reading a book?

"Or do you keep quiet and risk the whole place explodes?" It was a fact they lived with every day. "I almost crawled out of my skin before he came back, grabbed his bag and left." He cleared his throat but didn't look at her. "I never ate there again."

She imagined not. The walls closing in. The roof sinking lower. All focus on the abandoned bag she could almost see in her mind, even though he hadn't described it. "I wouldn't have eaten there again either." Morgan understood him, and he understood her. No one else ever had.

If they were as close as they used to be, she'd move to his side and lean into his shoulder, so great was the sagging feeling of relief his words brought. Here was Eric, a man in need, searching for his sister…saying the one sentence that was the balm to her lonely soul. "I was close enough to take shrapnel to the cheek, and I never saw the backpack." If she had, maybe those people would still be alive. Maybe her life wouldn't have run off the rails.

But then she wouldn't be here now. Somehow sitting in a cave with Eric, even with the grim circumstances surrounding them, was exactly where she was supposed to be.

Eric was watching her again and then he was beside her. He smoothed a wayward strand of hair from her cheek and lingered on the scars there, intent on watching his thumb lightly brush a circle over them. "I always wondered what happened, and you'd never tell me."

"I was afraid." She choked on the words, her voice strangled.

His touch froze, then his hand cupped her cheek as if he could somehow cover the scars and protect her from the past. "Of what?"

Now his eyes grabbed hers and held on, erasing the years between them.

Her voice was a breath, a whisper. "You'd leave."

The force of truth would have knocked her off her feet if she hadn't already been sitting. She'd allowed their marriage to fall apart, had let him walk away from her not because she didn't want to leave her job and her safe place in the canyon...but because her heart had never fully been his. She'd walled it in with fear he'd see the real her and abandon her in some random spot around the globe. He'd see weakness and shame her.

Like Kevin had.

Eric lifted his other hand and gently turned her to face him, not letting her look away. "Who hurt you?"

His touch made her heart beat faster, made her remember how she'd once loved this man yet had been unable to receive his love in return. She tried to pull away but he wouldn't let her. "I'm a coward."

"According to who? The guy before me? The idiot who let you go?" His voice was low and husky. "He was wrong. You spend weeks alone in some of the most dangerous country in America. You got to your feet and took charge after one of your worst fears came true and a bomb exploded in the park. You stood your ground when a man tried to kill me. No." He leaned forward until his lips whispered against her ear. "No. You're the bravest person I know." He brushed a light kiss over her scars, then rested his cheek against hers, warm and way too inviting. "I'm the coward, the other idiot who let you go."

She wanted to tell him he was wrong, but he was too close. He stole what was left of every argument she'd ever used to push him away. Something in the back of her mind said she should push him away again. They were in danger and his sister was still missing, but...

But she couldn't. The dormant part of her heart that loved him had started to beat again.

Instead of running, hiding, protecting her emotions, she tilted her head and let her lips brush his.

* * *

The shock of her butterfly-wing kiss almost rocked Eric backward. As many nights as he'd thought of her, remembered her, wondered how she was doing… He'd never, ever imagined he'd be in her presence again, let alone she'd kiss him again.

It completely ripped his world in two.

No, it didn't tear at his world. It almost killed him. His lungs refused to breathe. He should pull away, because if he accepted her kiss… If he returned her kiss… Then everything would change. Because with Morgan Dunham, a kiss wouldn't be just a kiss. It would be handing his heart and life to her until the day he died.

It would change everything and solidify the decision he'd been wrestling with for months.

A decision he now realized had very little to do with Hannah and everything to do with Morgan. The nagging idea to leave the army and join the Park Service was every inch about rebuilding his life with Morgan Dunham.

He made his choice. He kissed her, pouring his heart and his life into a gesture he hoped said what words never could. He still loved her. He had spent every day of his life regretting his decision to walk away from her. He would never put his career above her again.

In the moment, his restless mind settled for the first time in nearly a decade. His heart fell into rhythm.

And his whole life changed. He stopped fighting Morgan. Stopped fighting God.

He surrendered.

When he broke the kiss, he realized his fingers were damp with her silent tears. Eric moved to sit beside her and pulled her close.

Morgan swiped at her cheeks and rested her head on his shoulder.

Silence reigned for who knew how long. He didn't care to count. For one brief span of time, he was going to sit with the woman who had grabbed his heart eight years ago during the search for his parents. He was going to rest in this holy moment of hearing God's purpose for his life and of having no emotional barriers between Morgan and himself.

Because he had no idea what tomorrow would bring.

Morgan sniffed and straightened, pulling her head from his shoulder and her warmth from his side. "I came here because I wanted to hide, because I was scared. Because I wasn't good enough to be anywhere else."

He wanted to argue but sensed she needed to say more. Reaching for her hand, he laced his fingers through hers in silent support.

"I never let you love me. I refused to move with you and told you it was because of my career, but it was because I couldn't bear to be left again. If I pushed you away, if I had a reason for you to go, then it wouldn't be about me. It would be about the job. Somehow I thought it would hurt less." Her fingers tightened around his. "But it only made me wonder every day if I'd done the right thing. So I resented you. I got angry at you. I never realized checking casualty lists online every week and tracking your hikes through the canyon with Hannah every year…" She drew a shaking breath. "It all meant I never stopped…"

For the first time in his life, Eric was speechless. He wanted to tell her she'd never loosened her firm grip on his heart, but the words wouldn't come. Instead, he kissed her fingers and hoped the gesture would be enough.

"But you know what? Our timing is all wrong again."

Morgan's smile was resigned and sad as she pulled her hand from his, rising to walk to the small cave entrance. "And who's to say what we're feeling is even real? We could be reacting to the threat of death, to the pressure of the situation…"

Eric stood and started to argue that these feelings weren't new, but she talked over his objections. "We need to focus on finding Hannah and getting all of us out of here alive. We can worry about this later. Talk about it when everyone is safe and whoever is behind these attacks on us and the other rangers is in custody."

Eric eyed her, balling his fist against his thigh to stop an argument that might only push her further away. Was she being wise? Or was she once again running scared?

SEVEN

Morgan focused on the ground in front of her, each step methodical in the bluish moonlight. The skies had finally cleared during the day while they'd hidden in the cave, not speaking, trying to conserve energy and water.

Trying not to think about what might have been and what could be.

The moonlight was a blessing or a curse. They were several hundred yards off the route most backcountry hikers chose, and the ground was uneven and sometimes unstable. In the daylight it would be a tough hike. In near darkness, it was downright foolish, but it was the only way to keep them partially hidden and physically safe.

Though she'd cast emotional safety to the wind.

After their intense discussion—and ground-shaking kiss—they'd spent the rest of a very long day in near silence. They'd managed some rest, with Eric sleeping near the cave entrance and Morgan farther back against the cool rock wall.

Now, although it was dark and the hike was treacherous, she was glad to be in open air and moving again. The atmosphere in the cave had been still and heavy with the words they'd said.

Morgan was terrified of being abandoned again. What if her decision to let him leave had nothing to do with her job and everything to do with her emotions? The idea made the ground under her feet feel shakier than it already was. Talking to him, baring her soul to him, left a raw wound in her spirit, one she needed to hash out with God and with herself before she made any more rash decisions.

Still, even if her choices in her marriage were born from fear, she still had a life to consider. Following Eric around the world to various duty stations would make her dependent on him and would signal a long pause in—and possibly the end of—a career she'd spent a decade building. One she loved.

But did she love it more than she loved him?

Morgan had no idea where he was stationed now. Did she know anything about him? Her foot slipped into a hole, and Eric's hand caught her elbow. "You okay?"

Leaning into his grasp, Morgan rotated her ankle and lofted a prayer of thanks for sturdy hiking boots. An injury could prove deadly. "Yeah, it's…" She knelt, running her hands around the edges of the hole that had nearly taken her out. It was about two feet across and sloped gradually, about three inches deep at its center. It was more of a depression, but no canyon animal dug a perfectly circular hole like this one. No canyon animal could dig through rock like this.

But humans could.

Eric crouched beside her and scanned the immediate vicinity, likely vigilant for threats. "What's up?"

"I'm not sure, but it's not good." She grabbed his hand and pulled him forward, nearly toppling him into the hole before he caught his balance. Placing his hand on the rock at the base, she guided his fingers over what she'd felt. "Shovels can't cut into the rock like this. There are ridges here, possibly made with some sort of pickax. Someone scraped through the topsoil until they hit rock, then took some more hits for good measure."

Morgan released his hand and rocked back on her heels, making a slow survey of the area for what could be seen in the near darkness. It had rained quite a bit since the hole was dug, which explained the curvature at the sides. She'd guess someone had overnighted here, but no one in their right mind would try to camp on this awkward path along the side of the slope. They wouldn't even hike here.

"Think it's an old archaeological dig?" Eric mimicked her posture with his weight on his heels.

"No. Digs in the canyon are rare. The Park Service has a 'preservation in place' mandate. We protect artifacts where they are. Digs are only allowed if a site is threatened by erosion, to save any artifacts from being lost or destroyed." She tapped her finger against her knee. "It's been a few years since the last authorized dig. It was along the river when it became obvious the Glen Canyon Dam allowed for more erosion to jeopardize some sites." Bracing her hands on her knees, she stood, and Eric followed suit. "I don't know. It's probably nothing. Someone could have decided to make camp here or there could be another equally mundane explanation."

Eric wandered a few feet away, watching his steps. "I doubt it. There's too much of a slope and too many rocks. No good shelter, no good sleeping space. And it's too far from any workable campsite to be a latrine."

Yeah, she'd noticed. "I'll make my best guess of where we are and report it when we get communication, since there shouldn't be any digging in the canyon at all. But if this is the only spot, it was probably nothing."

"I hate to tell you it's not nothing." He stopped about five yards away, a blue silhouette in the moonlight, and aimed a finger to his right. "Here's another one."

She glanced at her watch, then at the sky. They had only a handful of hours before the sun would start its rise and they'd have to take shelter again. She wanted to be at the river by daybreak. "I know we should keep moving, but…"

"But you want to get an idea of how big of a problem you're dealing with?"

She nodded, and although he probably couldn't see it, he knew. In a quick fifteen minutes spent pacing off the area, they located seven more holes.

They were on the move again before Eric spoke from behind as she navigated the sloped trail. "What are you thinking?"

"Nothing good. Based on where we are, someone stole Hopi artifacts. There are protected spots in this area, and even though I don't have GPS or daylight to be sure, I'd say we aren't far from one of those spots." Nausea stopped the rest of her words. The idea of someone profiting off Native Americans' history was the height of disgusting.

Eric's footfalls ceased behind her. "Morgan?"

"Yeah?" She turned and found him stopped on the sloped rock, staring at her. "I could be a complete conspiracy theorist, but earlier we were discussing… Hannah could have been taken by someone."

The sick feeling sank deeper, sweeping through Morgan's bones. "And she's an archaeologist."

"One who specializes in Southwest Native American culture, particularly in and around the canyon. She'd never participate in an illegal dig, but this is her area of expertise. In fact, our first day on the trail, she was talking about hoping a dig would open in the canyon someday. What if..." He swiped the air as if to wipe the thought away, but it came to completion and hung in the silence between them.

What if someone knew who she was and was holding her against her will?

Pain washed through Eric in waves, starting in his stomach and running through his body to his fingers and toes. Pain that had nothing to do with this insane nighttime flight through the backcountry of the Grand Canyon.

The thoughts he'd managed to squash pounded him with every step. Hannah lost in the wilderness was one thing. She was resourceful, smart...

But Hannah in the hands of someone who was up to no good...

He bit back a groan trying to work its way from his gut. If there was an illegal dig in the canyon, and whoever was in charge was holding Hannah, then it was likely whoever pursued them was also involved in this jagged, lethal puzzle.

Which would mean Hannah was being held by someone who wasn't afraid to kill to get their way. They'd talked about a random stalker, but a targeted hit on Hannah and on them?

Which was scarier?

A deep, thundering roar throbbed in his head. It had started almost ten minutes earlier and seemed to grow louder with every step. Having run out of water a couple of hours earlier, he was probably in the early stages of dehydration, but it shouldn't be affecting him this severely.

Stress. Fear. Dehydration. Maybe the combination was all messing with his head.

Except it wasn't in his head.

The noise beat him from the outside. The roar of a hundred jet engines, rumbling in the distance, grinding on his already shredded nerves. The canyon was supposed to be silent, but this? This was incredible. "What is that sound?" His voice came out as harsh as the roar.

Morgan didn't seem to notice his tone when she glanced over her shoulder. At least, she didn't respond to it. "There are rapids on the Colorado where we're headed. Usually, they aren't this loud on approach, but the rain lately must have the river higher than I thought."

"Will your site be compromised?" The last thing they needed now, lost in the canyon with no water and little food, was to find the river was closed to rafters and had swept away their last hope for survival.

"It would take a five-hundred-year flood to wipe out where it's hidden, but if the river's high enough, it could be an interesting retrieval."

"So we'll get the cache and wait for a rafter to come along and radio for help like we planned."

"Yes."

"Except I want to change the plan." The thought had dogged him for the past hour. He had to rescue Hannah. He was her only hope.

Morgan stopped and, when Eric stepped alongside her, faced him head-on. "We're way past changing the plan."

"I can't leave with Hannah still out here, not if somebody's holding her hostage. Not if somebody's using her for an illegal dig."

"Conjecture. I never should have said it."

"You wouldn't have kept me from thinking it." Eric

dragged his hand over his head and down to squeeze the back of his neck. "Have them bring supplies in rather than take us out of here. We can keep looking, start being boots on the ground to some of the sites where there are known artifacts. We can—"

"You're forgetting someone has targeted us more than once. You need protection, too."

"I can handle it."

"Don't do this, Eric. Don't make me pull authority on you. We agreed on a plan." She held up her hand to stop him from speaking. "At this point, we both need medics to check us out, because we're pretty close to the danger zone. Even if we get water in the next hour, we still need to be cleared before we come out here again. I can't…" Morgan pulled in a deep breath as though she could fortify herself for what she was about to say. "I can't let you hurt yourself out here. Not when…" Her hand found his and she intertwined their fingers. "Not now."

She was ripping him in two. Everything she said made sense, but Hannah… He looked away and tried to extract his hand from hers, but Morgan held on. "Hannah needs me."

"She needs you alive and well." Lifting her other hand, she gently pressed his cheek, forcing him to look at her. "I know you want to rescue her. I know you want to find her. But sometimes you have to let go and let someone else be the hero. It can't always be you. 'I will lift up mine eyes unto the hills, from whence cometh my help. My help cometh from the Lord, which made heaven and earth.' It doesn't say her help comes from you."

Fire blew threw him. How dare she quote the Bible at him? And those verses no less? She had no idea what they meant to him, what—

"Our best option is to stay by the river and stick to the original plan. We can hitch a ride with a rafting party or use their gear to get a message out and help in. And, remember, I have to get word out sooner rather than later about someone digging, especially if—"

"Is that the most important part?" Eric jerked his fingers from hers, the full inferno of his anger burning in the dryness of his soul. "Letting them know your precious artifacts are in danger is bigger than finding my sister?"

"You didn't let me finish." Her voice hardened with an edge Eric had never heard before, but she couldn't possibly expect him to walk away when Hannah might be in greater danger than they'd thought. "I was going to say if we can convince someone Hannah might have been kidnapped, we might be able to get a broad search reinstituted. No one searched this area because it didn't seem she'd head this direction. It's a long shot, but walking out today gives us a better chance of finding her tomorrow."

She stepped closer to him and rested her palm on his cheek. "Will you trust me?"

That might be the problem. He did trust her. Trusted her with his life.

Whether he wanted to or not. This was Morgan. She'd said she still loved him, and that truth banked the fire raging in his emotions, though it did nothing to ease his pain. "I do, but it's not easy to return to civilization knowing she's out here." Not when she needed a rescuer.

"I know." Morgan turned and headed for the river, which roared louder. "If we don't do something to protect ourselves and bring help…" She picked her way along the slope.

Then all three of us are dead.

EIGHT

The day was creeping toward sunrise when they reached the river, the sky tinged a pinkish hue. They hiked in the open more than Morgan wanted, but it couldn't be helped. Forging a path from the creek bed had been a rough go all night, walking off center with one foot higher than the other on the rocky slope. Then they'd found those holes...

Whoever was digging was bold. Tourist planes and helicopters regularly flew over this area. They had to be running a small-scale excavation under some sort of cover, perhaps in the dark. While not brand-new, the holes were probably dug within the past month. It was possible whoever was behind them had found what they wanted and left.

Or they'd merely relocated.

Morgan had kept her fears about Hannah to herself, but Eric had latched onto them anyway. It wasn't much of a stretch. Having a local expert on-site would embolden anyone digging illegally. Hannah had done much of her doctoral research in the canyon and had been published. Anyone looking for information would eventually come across her name. But how would they have known when she would be in the canyon and where to find her?

Morgan stumbled over nothing and righted herself before Eric could reach out to her. If all of these random dots were truly connected and Hannah truly had been kidnapped, the perpetrator would almost have to be someone Hannah knew.

It was all so far-fetched, though. A missing hiker was one thing. An antiquities thief turned kidnapper and attempted murderer? That was the stuff of movies and TV shows.

The need for food and water must be getting to her. She'd already started developing a dull headache, having rationed her water a little too tightly. The sight of the Colorado River around the last bend had never been more welcome. The river tumbled through the rapids higher than usual, a foaming, churning mess. She wanted to dive in anyway and bury herself in cool water. To kneel at the edge, scoop it in her hands and drink.

Which would only lead to a whole lot more trouble. The thought of the aftermath of unpurified water made her stomach cramp.

She stopped a few feet from the river's edge and glanced up and down the canyon. The cache was about a hundred feet away in a crevice about five feet off the ground. A five-gallon survival can of fresh water and some MREs would save their lives.

Eric stood beside her, but he turned and faced the way they'd come, his eyes narrowed and scanning from left to right slowly, methodically.

Morgan fought the urge to turn around. "What?"

"Nothing. Just…" His gaze roamed high to low once more, then turned to the river. "I had this funky feeling the day Hannah disappeared and I have it again, but it's probably dehydration and adrenaline." Exhaling loudly, he shook his head. "Which way now?"

Pointing to the right, Morgan eyed their intended path in the growing light. The canyon was narrow here, but the unusually high water had made it even more so. Only about two good feet of walkable space stood between rocks and river.

"This could get tricky." Morgan dropped her bedroll. "We're going to have to edge along where the river is high. Toting water cans and a pack with MREs is going to take work. Worse, with the river this high, they may not be letting anyone raft. We could be sitting here for a couple of days." At least they had filtration kits and the hours to let water settle so it could be filtered. Dehydration wouldn't kill them, although something else might.

"Been thinking about ways to make contact." Eric's eyes took on their first spark of life since they'd left the shelter of the cave after sunset last night. "High water in the canyon won't stop tourist flyovers, right?"

"No. Why?"

"Well, the slope we walked along is only about twenty degrees and it climbs about fifteen hundred feet."

Morgan turned on her heel and eyed the path they'd traversed. The land sloped to a mesa over a thousand feet above them, and the angle wasn't horrible. "Totally awed by those math skills you pulled out of nowhere."

He actually winked. "Yeah, well, the army still believes in old-school orienteering. Drop you in the middle of nowhere, hand you a map and a compass and that's it. Get to Point Bravo by zero six hundred and have fun, soldier."

"So I should have been letting you take the lead all along?"

He offered a one-shouldered shrug. "The cans in MREs are highly reflective, right? So I say we eat breakfast, hydrate, then tackle the slope. As soon as the planes or helicopters are up, we'll be there with a signal mirror, ready to make contact."

Morgan gauged the route he suggested. His plan was doable, though it would put them in the open. She glanced at the river, then to the mesa. "It's risky, but it may be our only chance of getting help. If they're digging at night and we can get some thermal-imaging equipment in the air, things could get interesting."

"Sounds good. The quicker we get out of here, the quicker we return. So where's this cache?"

"About a hundred feet along that very narrow space between the river and the rocks. A bit above eye level. I'll get it and—"

"No, I'll get it."

Morgan dug her fingernails into her palms. She wasn't afraid of the river, and she wasn't some damsel in distress. She was a competent ranger who could take care of both of them. "I think I can handle a cache retrieval."

"I'm taller than you, and the idea of you stretching on your tiptoes above raging water isn't a pleasant one for me, okay?" He jabbed his finger downriver. "It might be tranquil there, but you know…"

Yeah, she knew. If she slipped while reaching, the current would sweep her past the small beach and into the rapids. While she'd seen people flip canoes and survive, she'd also witnessed the aftermath when someone didn't.

Including Eric's parents.

She blinked away sudden tears. There was no way he'd risk letting her fall. And there was no way she'd ask him to. The thought had to terrify him.

She gave a quick nod. "There should be a small triangle painted on the rock at about your eye level. The cache is in a cleft above it."

"Thank you for understanding." He hesitated, then planted a gentle kiss on her forehead. "I'll be back in a few."

He headed upriver and onto the narrow path at the edge, pressing against the rock to keep his feet from the edge, where loose rock could slide into the water and take him with it.

Morgan turned toward the trail behind her as a strange sensation crawled along her spine. No one was there. The path turned a few feet from the small beach, but there was no indication anyone had followed them. Eric's paranoia had infected her.

Walking to the water's edge, she watched Eric pull the food pack out and sling it onto his back, then heft one of the five-gallon plastic water cans out of the site. If he was smart, he'd grab one now and carry it two-handed in front of him, then return for the other. It would make balancing easier and would—

She heard a soft sound from behind, and then a force caught her in the small of the back, shoving her into the water.

She stumbled and hit with a splash, the chilled river water sucking the air from her lungs as she first went under, then fought to stand in the shallows. The water wasn't deep but it was cold, and the current tugged with unbelievable strength.

Morgan struggled to get to her feet, but the river sucked her legs from under her, dragging her on her back along the bottom, pulling her head beneath even rougher water. She tried to dig in with her fingers but the current ripped her away as rock tore at her nails. She had to stop. Had to get out of the current before...

Before the rapids. Before the jagged rocks that split and foamed the water.

Without a life jacket, she'd get sucked under and beaten to death.

The current zipped wildly, shoving, tossing. Water and sky tumbled. She lifted her head to gasp air, then went under again, fighting to keep her face to the surface as the river flipped and rolled.

Everything was numb. So cold. She needed air. Needed to stop moving, but everything jumbled together. Air and water. Pain and nothingness.

The cold, the water, the exhaustion... Blackness tinged the edges of the world, but she couldn't let it engulf her, couldn't give in to it. She had to fight.

Eric couldn't lose her to the river, too.

With a massive shove, she planted her feet and wedged them against the side of a rock, stopping her movement and sending a shot of adrenaline to her muscles. She'd done it!

But a shift in the current around the rock caught her shoulder and shoved her up and forward, toward the river and toward the rock. Her ankle wrenched. Her abdomen slammed into rock, sending her face-first into the water...

Into darkness.

"No!" The word tore from Eric's throat, shredded and raw.

His muscles locked. His mind froze.

All that existed was Morgan, bobbing limply down the river, the sound of her pained cry echoing in his mind as the rapids threw her.

Past. Present. His parents. Hannah.

Morgan.

Dropping the water can, he leaped in, his foot slipping into the water and soaking to his shin. Eric stumbled, recovered and raced as fast as he dared to the small beach, slinging the pack of food to the ground.

Morgan tumbled. She fought for the surface, gulped air and disappeared. Over and over. Again and again. In the fight for her life.

In a fight Eric couldn't win for her.

He ran into the water nearly to his knees. The strong current threatened to swamp him. He would be of no help to her if he hurled himself into the flow, trapped himself in the fast-moving water.

They'd both be dead.

He couldn't save her.

Eric's entire body wanted to cave. Too much death. Too much pain. Too much loss.

But Morgan...

I will lift up mine eyes unto the hills, from whence cometh my help. My help cometh from the Lord, which made heaven and earth.

He couldn't do nothing. He couldn't stand by and watch her race further away.

Forcing himself out of his emotions, he dug into his tactical mind. He had to reach her, but the rapids were in a narrow part of the canyon without a ledge on the sides. All that lay along the water was rocks. Slippery, wave-washed rocks.

He had to get to the far side of the rapids to the beach. He had to be there to reach out to her, to dive in and snatch her from the calmer waters before she drifted away again.

To rescue her.

"Lord, give me balance. Give her air. Keep her out of an eddy." He prayed through gritted teeth, terrified she'd be caught in a swirl and circled into eternity.

He leaped onto the nearest rock, slowly, wishing he could run, knowing to do so would sign both of their death warrants.

I will lift up mine eyes unto the hills, from whence cometh my help. My help cometh from the Lord, which made heaven and earth.

Was this how his father felt? Had he watched Eric's mother float away, helpless to save her? Had he dived in as the river stole them both?

He wavered on the slippery rocks. Only a hundred feet. The rapids were only a hundred feet. So short a distance. So far away.

Another rock. Another.

Where was Morgan?

There. Nearing the rapids' end, where the water swirled and threatened to trap her.

Not as long as he had breath in him.

His feet hit the beach and slid, his knee banging on slick rocks. With a shove, he ran through the pain and the fear until he was parallel with Morgan.

She was free from the rapids but her fight was gone. She floated on her back, tried to move her arms, but they seemed too heavy.

Eric had seconds before she sank a final time and the river ripped her away, never letting her surface again.

He ran into the river's edge until he was knee-deep, then dived, frigid water covering his head. The current was less severe here on the far side of the rapids, but it still fought to pull him off course and downriver from

Morgan. He surfaced, found her farther to his right and pushed with everything he had. Pushed with every tactic he'd learned in water training. Pushed until his muscles screamed in the icy water.

One more lift of the head, one more gasp for air, one more search for Morgan... There, so close. He altered course and dug in, mind over body. In one final heaving stroke, his hand found her shirt, his fingers closing around cloth.

He pulled her to him, turned on his back and fought for both of them. Fought the black that threatened to engulf his mind, his body and his heart. This was how he'd lost his parents. This was how their last moments had been lived, fighting the river, fighting for each other.

Fighting until the river won.

NINE

Morgan coughed, sputtered and tried to bring the world into focus. River and sky had tumbled for too long. Cold water had sapped her muscles of strength, her lungs of air...

Her body had betrayed her when an irresistible force pulled her to shore. Too tired to fight, too exhausted to help, she'd succumbed until Eric lowered her onto the smooth rocks beside the river.

She lay in the sun's growing warmth, eyes squeezed shut as darkness receded and early-morning light filtered in. All she wanted was air. And sleep.

Sleep was too much like the darkness she'd fought so hard. Morgan bolted up with a cry, gulping air, swinging her arms to fight the weight. She would not surrender, would not give in.

"Hey, whoa." Gentle arms encircled her, and pulled her to a strong chest, damp and chilled against her cheek. Eric.

"You're okay. You're safe. I've got you."

I've got you.

Tense, frozen muscles relaxed.

I've got you.

She'd never believed him before. Every time he'd told

her in the past, she'd been utterly convinced he was going to learn of her cowardice and leave her where she deserved to be…alone.

But he hadn't. She clutched the front of his damp shirt and buried her face in his neck, shaking from the inside out.

His arms tightened around her and they stayed there as the sun lifted higher and the blue sky brightened.

"Don't ever scare me like that again, woman." His voice was husky. He pressed a kiss to her forehead, then dropped onto the rocks beside her, breathing heavily. "I thought we were both gone."

"I'm sorry." She'd failed, had turned her back and missed the clues. Like in Kevin's club the night of the concert. She'd missed…

A gasp tore at her water-bruised lungs and shot pain through her side and into her left shoulder. "Someone… someone shoved me into the water." It surfaced with clarity, the memory submerged during her fight for survival. A blow to the back, a force driving her forward.

"What?" Eric scrambled to his feet, searching the area. "Are you sure?"

She nodded, the pain in her body a physical testimony. Everything ached from bruises and tension. Her shoulder and her left side protested every time she inhaled. "I didn't see them."

Eric clinched his fists, his mouth a grim line. "I shouldn't have left you alone. Not knowing we were—" He shook out his hands and knelt beside her. "We have to get out of here. They'll try again. At this point, our only way out is up. All of our gear is on the other side of the river and the rapids. It's a steeper climb on this side, but we have to signal an aircraft. There's no other way."

They had no food. No water. Morgan was battered and exhausted, and Eric likely was, too. The more she breathed, the more her side and shoulder protested. Something was wrong. Something she couldn't articulate.

It had to be fear, maybe a panic attack. That would make sense given all they'd been through.

Given all they still had to go through. Surviving the climb on a normal day would be challenging, even without the added danger of a killer nearby. Today?

They had no other choice but to try…and pray. Morgan nodded. It was time to be the woman she was, the one who stomped fear and survived in the wilderness. The ranger. "Faster we move, faster we have help." She reached for Eric's extended hand, loathe at needing help, but her muscles still shook. Her body was at its limit. If she made the hike, it would be by God's grace alone. "It's going to be—" Pain tore through her ankle as her weight landed on it.

Only Eric's grip on her hand and then under her arm kept her from crashing to the ground.

He knelt beside her and unlaced her waterlogged hiking boot. "What?"

Every motion brought pain. "Stop." Gritting her teeth as spots danced before her eyes and cold sweat broke on her skin, Morgan swiped at his hand, the memory of jamming her ankle against river rocks returning. "Don't take it off." If he touched her foot again, she'd either pass out or punch him.

Eric rocked onto his heels and stared into the distance, the thoughts in his head practically visible on his face.

They were likely as dark as her own. The reflected sunlight into the canyon was warm now, but it would quickly grow hot and dangerously direct as the day wore on. They were trapped on this beach, on the opposite side of the river from their survival gear. Even if Eric dared to attempt a swim, the rapids were still between them. A killer knew their location and wasn't afraid to exploit it.

There was no way Morgan could climb the mesa, and it was too steep for Eric to carry her.

From this angle, they'd reached the end of their line.

"You have to leave me here. Get to high ground and signal a helicopter or plane. They'll be flying over soon."

"No." Eric rose, insides quaking with adrenaline and hunger. With a shudder, he turned to eye the path to the mesa. It was steeper on this side, but still doable…for someone with two good ankles.

The choice was impossible. To make the climb to visibility meant leaving Morgan behind with the twin killers of man and nature. To stay and protect her meant a slow death with their gear in sight but out of reach.

A slow death for him meant certain death for his sister, as well.

Eric walked toward the river, more to give himself room to think than to seriously consider crossing.

The rocks on the far side had taken him only a minute, maybe two, to traverse but they were treacherous. Seeing them now, with his mind clearly focused on them and not on Morgan, it was clear God alone had gotten him over those without sliding him into the river to a water-soaked grave.

They were trapped. There was nothing he could do to save them.

"You can't quit now." Morgan's voice from behind him was stronger than it had been a few minutes earlier. She was regaining strength, but it wouldn't do a thing to help her ankle. "Hannah needs you. I need you."

Climbing to the mesa without her was contrary to everything he'd ever been trained to do. You didn't leave a man behind. You definitely didn't leave the woman you loved behind.

Eric whipped around and stared at her. She watched him, her eyes rimmed with dark circles, her hair drying in heavy curls.

He did still love her. He'd do anything to save her.

Even if *anything* meant leaving her behind?

Climbing or staying, either way, he could be killing her.

Unless… "You said rafters are pretty regular on the river?" He almost choked on the words. He knew the answer already, but it wasn't one he ever liked to think about, not after his parents…

"Four days ago there was talk of shutting it for a few days until the water levels dropped a bit. A couple of class nines and tens were on the verge of impassable, and that was before the last big washout we had. It's possible no one will come."

"How soon before we know?" If there was a chance he could summon help on the river, he'd take it.

"I don't know. Sun's been up about half an hour? Depends on how far upstream they made camp, what time they hit the river… Could be two hours before we can say for certain no one's rafting, but you're burning daylight during the wait. Not to mention extending your time without food and water. The longer you wait, the harder and more dangerous the climb is going to be."

He'd risk it. She could argue all she wanted but he couldn't leave her. His heart would kill him. "Say someone put in for the night close by and got an early start. We could know in...?"

"Less than half an hour."

Closing the space between them, he dropped to her side but kept his distance. She was right. He'd have to move soon or risk passing out as his body weakened and the day's heat kicked in. He already ached with the need for water. If he so much as held her hand, his resolve to hike out without her would waver.

Half an hour.

"You don't need to worry about me." Morgan stretched her legs and studied her injured ankle, which was puffing around the top of her boot. "Whoever shoved me in is on the other side of the river. It will take time for them to cross. I'll get out of sight by the rocks and no one will know I'm here." When he started to argue, she held up a hand. "No. Both of us need food and water more than we need to worry about someone coming at us. We'll die for sure without them. We only theoretically die any other way."

No matter what happened, it would be his fault. He was caught between a literal rock and a hard place, trapped with two other lives in his hands and no good way out.

He scanned Morgan's face, trying to formulate a plan, a perfect solution, some way to—

Her eyes widened and she straightened, focused on something over his shoulder. "Eric..."

He whipped around, ready to fight, but relief and shock quaked in his muscles.

On the river, a man and a woman angled an inflatable raft to take on the rapids.

They were saved.

TEN

As Eric helped the man haul the craft onto the small beach, the woman had a brief conversation with him, then jogged over to Morgan, her auburn ponytail bouncing. "I'm a nurse practitioner. Maybe I can take a look at your ankle?" She held out a large water bottle. "And offer you some of this? I hear your gear is on the other side of the river."

Normally, the thought of drinking out of someone else's container would make her gag, but the heat in Morgan's throat overrode her usual germ aversion. Cool water eased the burn.

Relief sagged muscles so tense, Morgan felt limp in the aftermath. Her brain fogged from her ordeal and pain in her abdomen threatened to swamp her, but it didn't matter. Rescue had come. They could radio out, hitch a ride with these folks to an open spot for an aircraft to come in... They could get eyes in the air looking for a possible illegal dig site...and for Hannah.

Their ordeal was over.

But Hannah's still continued.

Morgan blinked, then drank another long draft of water. One thing at a time. "Glad you guys came along."

She sat straighter as the woman knelt at her side and eyed her hiking boot. "If you've got a radio or any kind of satellite device, that would be great."

"There's one on the boat. Soon as I know you're stable, I'll get it to you. You're pretty banged up. Gonna have some killer bruises." The woman tugged her ponytail tighter and scanned Morgan's leg to her hip. Her brow furrowed. "You're carrying a gun?"

Her Glock. She hadn't checked to see if it survived the river dunking. Her hand went to her hip, where an empty holster met her fingers. It must have ripped away in the water, probably when she was dragged against the rocks.

Her entire body ached at the memory, the earlier release of tension allowing her muscles to feel. Everything throbbed, and the world felt like she still viewed it from underwater. She'd probably find a whole lot more injuries than her ankle, but now wasn't the time to worry about them. "I had one. It's at the bottom of the river now."

The woman nodded, then glanced over her shoulder at the man chatting with Eric on the bank. He seemed to catch her eye, then returned to his conversation.

Something about the exchange ran a chill through Morgan. Uh-oh. When she'd been on patrol in San Diego, she'd watched drug dealers send signals along the same way. A quick nod. A hand gesture. Enough to let the next guy know a cop was in the area without calling attention to themselves.

Maybe she was paranoid, but it seemed like a signal.

If only Eric would turn her way so she could send her own, but he was deep in conversation.

Morgan cleared her throat. Maybe she was wrong. Maybe having their gear stolen and Eric attacked and getting shoved into the river had skewed her judgment. Or maybe that vague feeling of wrong, as though her body was off-kilter, was playing with her head.

Maybe. "You don't like guns?"

"What?" The stranger stopped assessing Morgan's ankle and studied her face, seeming to gauge her thoughts.

Alarm bells rang in Morgan's head, forcing through the fog in her head to compete with the pain in her body. Something wasn't right, not with her and not with this woman. Wincing, she bent her knee and dragged her foot closer. "I'm surprised the river is open to rafters as high as it is right now."

"Park Service opened it this morning."

Morgan's insides iced over, an unwelcome addition to the growing pain in her shoulder and abdomen. There was no way they could have put in this morning and made it this far already. "You're lying." She never should have said that. Never should have tipped her hand.

With a half smile, the woman reached behind her back and drew a pistol, rising to stand over Morgan with an unwavering aim at her forehead. "You're a hard woman to kill, Ranger."

"Morgan!"

Eric's cry only drew a higher tilt of the lip from the woman in front of her. "You have him?"

"Yeah." Behind her, the man who'd piloted the boat leveled a pistol on Eric, who held his hands out to the sides but was watching Morgan.

They were helpless again. Trapped again. Fear threatened to burn Morgan alive, but she lifted a prayer and choked it down. God had gotten them out of more than one mess this week. He could get them out of this one, too. Somehow. He had a way of making a path even when she didn't see one. Like Eric's verse, her help didn't come from anywhere but Him.

They sure did need Him now.

The woman nodded. "Get him in the boat. I'll handle our ranger friend and then we can get moving." She tilted her head as though considering Morgan, her eyes cold.

There would be no hope of begging for her life now.

The barrel of the pistol pressed into Morgan's forehead, hard and cold.

"Don't worry. It will all be over before you know it."

They were going to kill Morgan. Right in front of him.

There wasn't time to take out his captor and make it across the small beach fast enough to keep Morgan's assailant from pulling the trigger. He was helpless to keep her alive.

Helpless. Like his father before him.

Now he'd really failed.

Lord, give me something. Anything.

The man tossed a set of zip tie handcuffs at Eric's feet. "Put them on one wrist. I'll handle the other as soon as my partner is done with her part of the job."

Her part of the job. Killing Morgan. Killing Morgan while Eric watched, restrained and helpless.

Wait. If they were restraining him, then they didn't plan to kill him. These people clearly wanted him alive, while Morgan was expendable. He had special importance to whatever they were doing.

If they were really holding Hannah, maybe he was their leverage. She'd never willingly participate in an illegal dig, but if she thought Eric was in danger...

Eric stiffened his spine and looked straight into the

eyes of the man who held his life in his hands. "I won't cooperate if you kill her."

There was a flash of concern, then the man lifted the weapon higher. He stood out of Eric's reach, but a brief flicker of uncertainty replaced his cold determination. "What makes you think you aren't getting a bullet right after hers?"

"Because you need me." Boy, was this a long shot. He prayed he was right. "You have my sister, and she won't cooperate with you if I'm dead. You have nothing without me." Dots connected. Puzzle pieces clicked. That was why he was still alive. "You've come at me from fourteen different angles since I started to search for her, but not to kill me. It's all been to show Hannah what you *could* do if she didn't help you. Am I right?"

The man's Adam's apple bobbed once, surging a feeling of triumph through Eric. "So here's the deal. You kill the ranger, I come at both of you and give you no choice but to kill me. If I'm dead, you lose your cooperative expert. Then what are you going to do?"

A flicker of uncertainty in the man's eyes told him he'd guessed everything correctly. Without him, Hannah wouldn't cooperate.

In his peripheral vision, the woman stood, facing him but keeping her sidearm tight to Meghan's forehead. "This is getting too complicated. Too much extra weight. It's a snowball."

Not half as complicated as it was about to get, if Morgan would meet his eye and receive the signal he was sending.

She looked up. Held his gaze. Glanced at the pistol and the woman who was foolish enough to get within arm's reach of a trained ranger and then turn her back.

With the slightest motion, Morgan's chin dipped, then she pulled her good knee to her chest, preparing to launch on his signal.

The timing would have to be exact. They had two guns in play and either of them could fire in the struggle and hit someone.

It was a risk they had to take.

Their captors were intent on a conversation Eric could hardly hear over the roar of adrenaline in his body. Eric and Morgan had to move now, before their focus shifted to the business at hand.

With a quick prayer and a quicker nod, Eric dived at the man, who'd inched a bit too close, letting his gun get into Eric's reach. With his right hand, Eric twisted the man's wrist away while his left palm drove into the man's chin, causing him to stumble backward to the ground, the gun dropping as he fell.

It was a blur of seconds. Before his mind could process his actions, Eric was standing several feet from and above his former captor, pistol leveled at his chest. "Don't even flinch." A quick glance said he shouldn't have bothered to speak. The guy was out, flat on his back.

It wouldn't last more than a minute, though. He whipped to the side, weapon at the ready.

Morgan had apparently landed a solid upper kick to the other woman's knee, enough to knock her off balance and cause her to drop the pistol. But the woman was already heading for Morgan, who was still defenseless on the ground.

Eric fired a round into the air. "I wouldn't take another step unless you want the next one to hit its target."

The woman froze, hands reflexively lifting.

"Now move over here."

Behind him, the man groaned. Eric was running out of time. There was no way he could subdue two of them if they turned on him and, from the glean in the woman's eye, she knew it. "Morgan? Gun?"

"I've got it."

He glanced over to see her leverage herself against the rock and rise on her good foot, pistol leveled. She was pale and shaking. The gun wasn't going to hold aim for long.

With Morgan's backup, he retrieved the zip ties from the ground and restrained the woman. He used her shoelaces to bind her feet to her hands, then fashioned field handcuffs and restrained the man, as well.

With the threat neutralized, he jogged over to Morgan and she sagged against him as though her entire body had abandoned the fight. Something more was going on with her than the busted ankle. Maybe she was going into shock. He helped her to the boat, where he settled her into a seat. Her face was pale, her skin clammy. "You going to make it?"

She nodded once, sinking against the side of the boat and closing her eyes. "Just find their radio. Get us out of here." She spoke through gritted teeth.

The words shot through him. Eric was where he longed to be, where he was most comfortable...in charge.

Except he wasn't. In reality, he'd done nothing to save them. He had only responded to the situations at hand. At no point had he formulated and put a plan into action.

But God had.

It wasn't Eric's job to save. It was his job to surrender and obey. In this case, to use what he had at hand to move forward.

He had a job to do, not an operation to take charge of.

It took only two seconds to find the radio in a side pouch of a backpack lashed into the boat. He passed Morgan the radio and a water bottle, took a long, satisfying swig from a second container, then turned to the two who were trussed on the beach.

As Morgan called for help, Eric returned to the only link he had to Hannah's location. The man was still groggy, so Eric turned to the woman. "Where's my sister?"

"She's restrained at the dig site. Alone. Helpless."

Anger surged, hot and muddy through his veins. If she was telling the truth, Hannah could die if these two refused to talk while in custody. "Tell. Me. Where."

The woman smirked and turned her head away.

No. He couldn't come this close only to have her die… "I asked you a question."

"And I'm not answering." She met his eye, defiant to the end. "You won't shoot me. If you were going to, you'd have already done it. And if you do, you'll never find her. You have nothing. No leverage at all."

"Eric!"

He spun at Morgan's feeble shout and stepped to the boat, keeping one eye on their prisoners.

"Helicopter on the way. They'll land above us, work their way down. Even better…" She held up a small device. "GPS. There are coordinates entered. I think it's the…the dig site." She pulled a waterproof map closer and weakly jabbed a finger at a spot less than a mile downriver, at the top of another mesa. "I passed the intel along. A team's going…going in."

Eric turned and looked down at the woman who'd been taunting him only moments before. Gone was the defiance. In its place, worry reigned.

They'd found Hannah. "What's the ETA on help?" He didn't want to leave these two where they could escape, but his entire being strained to find his sister and get both Hannah and Morgan to safety.

He returned to the boat. Morgan looked even paler than she had before. He lifted his eyes to the sky and listened. In the distance, beyond the rise above them, the blessed sound of helicopter rotors grew louder. "They're almost here. It's almost over."

"Half a mile. Half a mile to Hannah." Morgan shifted and planted herself in the boat, wincing as she laid a hand on her left side. "Smooth sailing. No rapids to navigate. We should go. We have their weapons."

Eric eyed their subdued attackers. They should stay here and make certain the pair was taken into custody.

He turned to scan the placid waters downriver. But his sister...

Even if he could get to the scene, he still wouldn't be able to save her. Morgan would never be able to make the climb, and he wouldn't leave her. Even if they beat the helicopters to the top, at best, they'd be in the way. At worst, his interference could get someone killed.

No. He had to stay in place. Had to trust that his help really did come from the Lord.

As though his tortured thoughts were heard, the roar of rotors grew louder, and a helicopter settled on the mesa above them in a cloud of dust and dirt. Two more thundered overhead. One hovered near the bend in the river, exactly where Morgan had indicated the dig site should be. The other disappeared, likely settling on the ground. *Please, God. Let Hannah be alive.*

Ropes dropped down the canyon walls and a swarm of rangers rappelled to the bottom. Eric watched until their feet hit the beach, then turned toward the two downriver. What was going on? Did they have Hannah?

While one ranger climbed into the boat beside Morgan, another approached Eric. "It's good to see you're safe, Staff Sergeant. Let's get you geared up and out of here."

"I can't. Not until I know…" He'd left once while Hannah was still lost in the wilderness. He couldn't do it again.

The ranger's jaw hardened. He moved to speak, but the radio on his shoulder crackled to life. "We've got her. She's safe. Evaccing now."

It was over. Hannah was safe. Morgan was safe. Now they could—

"Chavez." The sharp call turned Eric and the ranger both toward the boat. The ranger with Morgan cut a hard look at his partner.

Morgan met Eric's gaze, but it was as though she saw right through him. Her mouth opened, her eyes widened in panic and she grabbed at the ranger's arm. Suddenly, she went limp against the boat, slipping to the side.

ELEVEN

Morgan blinked her eyes open, then closed them again. They were so heavy. In the distance, there were voices, footsteps… Smells assaulted her senses. Antiseptic. Medicinal.

Hospital? She forced her eyes open and tried to turn her head. Why was she here?

Where was Eric?

"Hey, beautiful." There was a rustle, the sound of something scraping on the floor, then he was beside her, his hand sliding gently under hers. "Thought you'd sleep all night."

"What time is it?"

"Around six in the evening. You've been sleeping since they brought you out of surgery." He swept hair off her forehead, then shifted so she could see him beside the bed.

He was clean-shaven, freshly showered and dressed in a Denver Broncos T-shirt. How long had she been asleep? "What surgery?"

His thumb drew lazy circles on her hand. "You ruptured your spleen. Had some internal bleeding, but the surgeons repaired it. It's a good thing our would-be kidnappers came along when they did or…" He cleared his throat. "You're safe."

Fumbling, Morgan found the buttons and raised the head of the bed a bit. An IV pumped fluids into her hand. Her foot was heavy with wrappings and elevated at the end of the bed. "Did I break it?"

"Bad sprain. It'll heal fast. As for your spleen…" Eric arched an eyebrow. "You'll be on light duty for a while."

Right now, she didn't care about duty, only about sleep.

She studied Eric instead. Something about him was… different. In the set of his jaw. In the look in his eye. He looked… Peaceful.

Which meant… "Hannah?"

"She's asleep up the hallway." His smile brightened. "They raided the camp and rescued her. Our two 'friends' left her alone there overnight to come after us. I knew I recognized the guy. He was one of her former class-mates. He's been smuggling antiquities for months, but he'd exhausted the locations he knew about and brought Hannah in to point him to more. Took some shots at me to show her he could. Took some shots at the rangers to keep them busy on the rim and away from the search for Hannah in the canyon."

It was a diabolical plan, and it had nearly worked. "Why aren't you with her?" He should be with the sister he'd believed in, searched for, prayed for… "You need to be with her."

Eric's fingers tightened on hers. "I told her everything while you were in surgery. She knows we were married, and she's a hopeless romantic who thinks I'm still in love with you and should be by your side." He swallowed and his dark gaze pinned hers. "She's right."

The jolt of his words spiked her heart monitor. Eric's grin said he noticed.

But she'd failed him. "I tried to get you to leave Hannah behind." Safety had motivated her. How was that any different from running from crowds?

He was bound to realize she was weak. The light that had dawned in his eyes the past few days would snuff out.

He leaned closer, his face hovering near hers. "We'd have died out there on our own. Your calls were right, rational. Mine were emotional and… And, well, prideful."

When she dared to meet his gaze, it was gentle, though a hint of steel lurked behind it. "Morgan, you did everything right." He planted a kiss on her forehead. "I don't know what kind of number your ex did on you, but you're stronger than you think. Also, you need to quit beating up the woman I love."

He didn't blame her. Didn't call her a mistake or a coward.

He loved her.

How was that possible?

"Sweetheart—" he planted a gentle kiss on her forehead "—you are the bravest person I know. There is no one I'd rather have beside me out in the wild. We're alive because you took charge and faced things that would send most people running for their lives. So what if crowds bother you? You're not a coward. I'd like to find that ex of yours and have a man-to-man talk with him for messing with your head."

"I divorced you because I was scared of losing you. I should have gone with you."

Eric drew his lips between his teeth and studied her. "Would you do things differently today?"

As she looked him in the eye, she knew she would.

Fear had kept her from a good man, who loved her. Never again. The Park Service would find a place for her near him. If it didn't, she'd find another way to make a living.

She needed to surrender her life fully to Christ, which meant not letting fear dictate her decisions. She ran her tongue along her teeth. "I'd—"

"Well, look who's awake." A nurse stepped into the room. "We were at the nurses' station wondering if you were going to sleep until tomorrow."

Eric dropped a quick wink, then settled in his seat.

This conversation wasn't over. In fact, it was just beginning.

Go figure he'd find her here.

Eric pulled into the small lot at the tucked-away overlook and parked next to Morgan's SUV.

She stood at the railing, the moments before sunrise illuminating her in a way that reminded him how much he wanted to spend the rest of his life with this woman.

Grabbing the envelope from the passenger seat, he ran his thumb along the edge. Yeah. This was right.

When he slammed the Jeep's door, she glanced over her shoulder and smiled. "Didn't expect to see you until later. Shouldn't you be packing?"

His leave was over in two days, and his flight took off early tomorrow morning. Packing could wait, though. All he had was a couple of duffel bags. "Shouldn't you be resting?"

It had been over a week since she'd been discharged. A week she'd spent chafing at not being able to drive, at being treated like an invalid, at being hovered over by both Eric and Hannah as she recovered from the injury that had nearly taken her life. It would be months before she could return to full duty.

She'd chafed at that, too.

But the week had given Eric and Morgan time to get to know each other again when their lives weren't in the balance. Time for Hannah to come to grips with the fact her brother had once been married…and, as he'd told her yesterday, wanted to be married again.

"You knew I'd be out here as soon as the doctor cleared me to drive."

Yeah, he knew. It was her favorite spot on the rim, a hidden overlook that allowed for a wide view of the sunrise. They'd spent more than one morning here together in the past.

Eric stuffed the envelope into his hip pocket and leaned his forearms on the rail next to her, their shoulders touching. For long minutes, they said nothing as the world held its breath and the sun slipped over the horizon, changing everything.

Kind of like God had changed him…when he really did send help from the hill above them. Like he'd changed Morgan when she finally realized she could trust in God's love and Eric's love without fear of being abandoned.

When it was too bright to face the sun any longer, Eric turned and leaned his hip on the rail, watching her. There was so much he wanted to say, but it stuck in his chest behind a knot of uncertainty. He was about to announce a major life change, one that affected her, as well.

She'd either accept or reject him.

Morgan watched him from the corner of her eye. "You've got an 'I know something you don't' look."

He probably did. How in the world was he speechless?

Without flourish, he pulled the envelope from his pocket and handed it to her.

She turned it over, then faced him with an eyebrow raised. "What's this?"

He could say "Open it and see," but he wanted to speak the words. "I'm getting out of the army."

Her expression danced from joyful to incredulous to sad before she reset it to concern. Her forehead drew into deep lines and she returned the unopened envelope. "You can't do this for me. You'll resent me. I can't ask—"

"It's not for you." He shoved the envelope into his pocket and took her hand. "Day one out here with Hannah, before everything went south, I realized I want to serve differently. I'm tired. I'm losing myself. I want to…" He dragged his free hand over his head. He was doing this wrong. "I'm happiest here. In the canyon. I want to be with family… With you." Did she grasp what he meant?

Morgan stopped breathing and her eyes widened, lifting her eyebrows above her sunglasses. "What are you saying?"

"It will take a few months, but I'm getting out. I've applied with the Park Service." He squeezed her hand. "Not because of you. Not for you. For me. You being here is a bonus."

She swallowed hard. "Because you want to start a family."

"With you. I love you."

"And I love you." Her lips drew between her teeth and she eyed him for a long moment before she straightened and cleared her throat. "You know, I haven't heard a question."

Slipping both arms around her waist, Eric pulled her

to him and rested his forehead against hers. "Marry me again, Dunham."

"That wasn't a question." The words were whispered and choked, but her arms slipped around his waist and gave him the answer he was looking for.

"*Will* you marry me again, Dunham?"

She tilted her chin until her lips brushed his and whispered, "One last time. For the rest of my life."

* * * * *

Dear Reader,

The craziest things happen when you write a book. You think you know where you're going, then God steps in. I thought we were going to trace Morgan's journey out of fear, but the deeper I dived, the more the story was about Eric. Initially, he was going to be the hero who saved everybody, but I realized sometimes being the hero means understanding you can't be the savior. See, we can believe in God. We can know Jesus died to save us. We can have knowledge yet lack surrender. We want to work our own plan. That was what Eric was doing. He was going to save everybody, but, in the end, he couldn't even save himself.

In that moment, he became a hero. His arrogance, cockiness and self-reliance were stripped away, and he realized he had to trust God. Surrender isn't a bad thing when it's surrender to God. Jesus never asked us to do anything for salvation other than believe salvation comes through Him alone. Like Eric, we have to drop our self-protective (and sometimes self-righteous) stance and tell Jesus, "I can't do a single thing to redeem myself. It's all You." That's the moment salvation begins. Actually, that's the moment when real freedom hits and that weight goes away. I'd love to hear from you. You can find ways to contact me at www.jodiebailey.com. I'm praying for you, and I'm so glad you hiked the Grand Canyon with me!

Jodie Bailey

**WE HOPE YOU ENJOYED
THIS BOOK FROM**

LOVE INSPIRED SUSPENSE
INSPIRATIONAL ROMANCE

Courage. Danger. Faith.

Find strength and determination in stories
of faith and love in the face of danger.

6 NEW BOOKS AVAILABLE EVERY MONTH!

COMING NEXT MONTH FROM
Love Inspired Suspense

Available May 5, 2020

CHASING SECRETS
True Blue K-9 Unit: Brooklyn • by Heather Woodhaven

When Karenna Pressley stumbles on a man trying to drown her best friend, he turns his sights on her—and she barely escapes. Now Karenna's the only person who can identify the attacker, but can her ex-boyfriend, Officer Raymond Morrow, and his K-9 partner keep her alive?

WITNESS PROTECTION UNRAVELLED
Protected Identities • by Maggie K. Black

Living in witness protection won't stop Travis Stone from protecting two orphaned children whose grandmother was just attacked. But when his former partner, Detective Jessica Eddington, arrives to convince him to help bring down the group that sent him into hiding, agreeing to the mission could put them all at risk.

UNDERCOVER THREAT
by Sharon Dunn

Forced to jump ship when her cover's blown, DEA agent Grace Young's rescued from criminals and raging waters by her ex-husband, Coast Guard swimmer Dakota Young. Now they must go back undercover as a married couple to take down the drug ring, but can they live to finish the assignment?

ALASKAN MOUNTAIN MURDER
by Sarah Varland

After her aunt disappears on a mountain trail, single mom Cassie Hawkins returns to Alaska...and becomes a target. With both her life and her child's on the line, Cassie needs help. And relying on Jake Stone—her son's secret father—is the only way they'll survive.

HOSTAGE RESCUE
by Lisa Harris

A hike turns deadly when two armed men take Gwen Ryland's brother hostage and shove her from a cliff. Now with Caden O'Callaghan, a former army ranger from her past, by her side, Gwen needs to figure out what the men want in time to save her brother...and herself.

UNTRACEABLE EVIDENCE
by Sharee Stover

It's undercover ATF agent Randee Jareau's job to make sure the government's 3-D printed "ghost gun" doesn't fall into the wrong hands. So when someone goes after scientist Ace Steele, she must protect him...before she loses the undetectable weapon *and* its creator.

LISCNM0420

SPECIAL EXCERPT FROM

HQN

*Return to River Haven, where a mysterious stranger
will bring two lonely hearts together…*

*When Amish quilt shop owner Joanna Kohler finds an injured
woman on her property, she is grateful for the help of fellow store
owner Noah Troyer, who feels it's his duty to aid, especially when
danger draws close.*

*Read on for a sneak peek at
Amish Protector by Marta Perry*

Home again. Joanna Kohler moved to the door as the small bus that connected the isolated Pennsylvania valley towns drew up to the stop at River Haven.

Another few steps brought her to the quilt shop, where she paused, gazing with pleasure at the window display she'd put up over the weekend. Smiling at her own enthusiasm for the shop she and her aunt ran, she rounded the corner and headed down the alley toward the enclosed stairway that led to their apartment above the shop.

The glow of lamplight from the back of the hardware store next door allowed her to cross to the yard to her door without her flashlight. Noah Troyer, her neighbor, must be working late. Her side of the building was in darkness, since Aunt Jessie was away.

Joanna fitted her key into the lock, and the door swung open almost before she'd turned it. Collecting her packages, she started up the steps, not bothering to switch on her penlight. The stairway was familiar enough, and she didn't need—

Her foot hit something. Joanna stumbled forward, grabbing at the railing to keep herself from falling. What in the world…? Reaching out, her hand touched something soft, warm, something that felt like human flesh. She gasped, pulling back.

Clutching her self-control with all her might, Joanna grasped her penlight, aimed it and switched it on.

A woman lay sprawled on the stairs. The beam touched high-heeled boots, jeans, a suede jacket. Stiffening her courage, Joanna aimed the light higher. The woman was young, *Englisch*, with brown hair that hung to her shoulders. It might have been soft and shining if not for the bright blood that matted it.

Panic sent her pulses racing, and she uttered a silent prayer, reaching tentatively to touch the face. Warm…thank the *gut* Lord. She…whoever she was…was breathing. Now Joanna must get her the help she needed.

Hurrying, fighting for control, Joanna scrambled back down the steps. She burst out into the quiet yard. Even as she stepped outside, she realized it would be faster to go to Noah's back door than around the building.

Running now, she reached the door in less than a minute and pounded on it, calling his name. "Noah!"

PHMPEXP0420

After a moment that felt like an hour, light spilled out. Noah Troyer filled the doorway, staring at her, his usually stoic face startled. "Joanna, what's wrong? Are you hurt?"

A shudder went through her. "Not me, no. There's a woman…" She pointed toward her door, explanations deserting her. *"Komm, schnell."* Grabbing his arm, she tugged him along.

By the time they reached her door, Noah was ahead of her. "We'll need a light."

"Here." She pressed the penlight into his hand, feeling her control seeping back. Knowing she wasn't alone had a steadying effect, and Noah's staid calm was infectious. "I was just coming in. I started up the steps and found her." She couldn't keep her voice from shaking a little.

The penlight's beam picked out the woman's figure. It wasn't just a nightmare, then.

Noah bent over the woman, touching her face as Joanna had done. Then he turned back, his strong body a featureless silhouette.

"Who is she?"

The question startled her. "I don't know. I didn't even think about it. I just wanted to get help. We must call the police and tell them to send paramedics, too."

Not wasting time, Noah was already halfway out. "I'll be back as soon as I've called. Yell if…" He let that trail off, but she understood. He'd be there if she needed him.

But she'd be fine. She was a grown woman, a businesswoman, not a skittish girl. Given all it had taken her to reach this point, she had to act the part.

Joanna settled as close to the woman as she could get on the narrow stairway. After a moment's hesitation, she put her hand gently on the woman's wrist. The pulse beat steadily under her touch, and Joanna's fear subsided slightly. That was a good sign, wasn't it?

The darkness and the silence grew oppressive, and she shivered. If only she had a blanket… She heard the thud of Noah's hurrying footsteps. He stopped at the bottom of the stairs.

"They're on their way. I'd best stay by the door so I can flag them down when they come. How is she?"

"No change." Worry broke through the careful guard she'd been keeping. "What if she's seriously injured? What if I'm to blame? She fell on my steps, after all."

"Ach, Joanna, that's foolishness." Noah's deep voice sounded firmly from the darkness. "It can't be your fault, and most likely she'll be fine in a day or two."

Noah's calm, steady voice was reassuring, and she didn't need more light to know that his expression was as steady and calm as always.

"Does anything get under your guard?" she said, slightly annoyed that he could take the accident without apparent stress.

"Not if I can help it." There might have been a thread of amusement in his voice. "It's enough to worry about the poor woman's recovery without imagining worse, ain't so?"

"I suppose." She straightened her back against the wall, reminding herself again that she was a grown woman, owner of her own business, able to cope with anything that came along.

But she didn't feel all that confident right now. She felt worried. Whatever Noah might say, her instinct was telling her that this situation meant trouble. How and why, she didn't know, but trouble nonetheless.

Don't miss what happens next in
Amish Protector *by Marta Perry!*
Available April 2020 wherever HQN books and ebooks are sold.

HQNBooks.com